Acknowledgments

Thanks to Chuck Roames, who gave me my start writing columns and loved the newspaper business, and who now owns a baseball card shop. To my editors, to Kathy Des Jardins, and most of all to Joan Swenson who excoriates my columns on a too regular basis. To Bob Bentley and Bob Johnson at The Californian, who gave me the go-ahead on this project. To my four children, Katie, Herbie, Sam and Thomas, who have inspired many of the portraits in this book and who, thank goodness, don't read me too closely yet. And finally to my wife, Sue, who thinks I'm a much better writer than I really am.

Table Of Contents

Foreword

Every city needs a newspaper columnist, just as every city needs a newspaper. The columnist goes beyond the hard edges of the news. He has the freedom to write about the city's life as seen through the eyes of one of its citizens. He makes it seem human. He reduces its institutions to the human level. He makes it come alive.

Herb Benham is the Bakersfield Californian's columnist. Though he writes of and for Bakersfield, his themes are universal. He reminds its citizens that all are human, like him. He is their mirror.

As a columnist myself, I know the rewards and disadvantages of the job. You make friends. Readers write to say that you have made them understand their city. You make enemies. They call you stupid; absurd, a racist, a sexist, an illiterate fool. There is almost no word a columnist can write that does not fall on somebody's foot.

Herb Benham surely has provoked all these responses in his column. But I suspect that in the long run he is appreciated. People love him, because they see in him their own hopes, frustrations, dilemmas and minor victories.

Benham has the proper credentials to be a Bakersfield columnist. He was born in Santa Barbara, but his father moved his family from that garden of earthly delights to Bakersfield when

Herb was one year old. Now 38, he has lived here ever since. He attended South High School. He and his wife, Susan, have four children.

As I did, he grew up in Bakersfield's summer heat and winter fog. He found that it was a place he could live and work and love in and in which he could raise a family. His column naturally is full of the daily delights and despairs of life in the Valley.

We find him at that most excruciating of social events, the 20-year high school reunion, meeting and dancing with the out-of-reach high school vamp he had never dared ask for a date.

We share his feelings of courage and cowardice when a bear peeks into his tent during a camping trip at Quaking Aspen with a friend and their three sons.

We bear witness to his feeling of ineptitude when he discovers a rat in his plum tree. These are the small adventures that householders face everywhere.

We experience with him his sense of awe, anxiety and helplessness when his wife goes into labor and he gets her to the hospital with only 35 minutes to spare.

He shares his joy in the upcoming marriage of an older sister who first called him a "chauvinist," introduced him to feminism and told him he ought to help his mother cook. "I cooked cheese souffle for 48 straight weeks."

We sympathize with his mixed feelings about a son who sucks his thumb. Despite the dire warnings of his friends, he finds something appealing about the habit.

It is not enough, however, to write a column about life's everyday trials and triumphs. The columnist is obliged to write with style, so that his humble pieces are in fact essays of literary quality.

This is the quality that Herb Benham has in abundance. His modest pieces are written with humor, grace and elegance.

It is those qualities that make them worth reading in the first place, worth remembering, worth re-reading, and worth collecting in a volume such as this.

- JACK SMITH.

Video camera

The day you buy a video camera is the day your kids stop being cute. We bought one. Our decision was accelerated by a gnawing feeling that the children were growing up and precious moments were being lost forever.

Remember those bits of time? They include the baby's first steps and his first bites of solid food. Impromptu plays, elaborate forts made with blankets and old cardboard boxes, and the upside-down parties. The times when kids veer off the deeply grooved path that we have worn for them and, against our better wishes, celebrate life the way they prefer.

So we bought a video recorder. A cute little guy. Afterwards, we drove home as fast as we could so we could capture the next original thing the kids did.

The first surprise was a notice along with the receipt advertising a video class at the store. I didn't need no stinking video class. I had seen enough guys with cameras on their shoulders to know that using one wasn't hard. Anyway, I wanted a camera, not another reminder of how obsolete my kind of intelligence was becoming.

We got home from the store and settled into the living room to put together our treasure. The kids were bouncing around like super balls. We were one big, happy family.

"Maybe you ought to look at the owner's manual," Sue suggested.

That's probably not a bad idea. Pick up a few tips. Sharpen my skills.

The manual was 157 pages long. It was thicker than the one that came with our car.

"I don't think we need this, honey," I said, flipping through the plump book. "This is pretty basic stuff."

I turned to the handwritten instructions the store owner had sent home with us. One of the first steps was to slide the battery on the rear of the camera so that we had power.

I tried to slide it on. It wouldn't slide. Maybe it required a tad more elbow grease. No progress. Maybe I just had to muscle it.

Still, no luck. Did we need glue? Twine? Finally the battery slid on. We had been sitting there 20 minutes and we had gotten to Step 2.

The kids danced through the room. "Are you ready to take our picture?" they said wildly. "We have a show for you."

Oh you do, do you?

"Get out of here," I barked. "We'll call you when we're ready."

Fifteen minutes later, we thought we were ready. Sue was going to do the first honors. "OK, kids, each of you tell us what your names are and how old you are," she said.

"Shoot, it's not working. There is a

red rectangle in the corner," muttered the distraught camera operator. "We spent all this money and it won't work. If I get discouraged, I don't know how much I'll use this thing."

Sue was becoming despondent. I wondered if the class included therapy for buyers with post-purchase depression.

I looked at the handwritten instructions. We had completed items one through five. I picked up the manual. Everything checked out.

I looked at the camera. What was wrong with this thing? I peered into the other end of the lens.

H'mmm, might help if we took off the old lens cap.

The camera has been fully operational for the last two weeks. We have 4 minutes and 31 seconds of screaming children jumping up and down, Sam stomping on cockroaches, and some unforgettable footage of the neighborhood children's orange stand, where all participants were suddenly struck mute and dumb.

Every time the kids do something really cute, the camera is two rooms away and neither of us wants to get up to get it. Every time we switch it on, the kids start acting like kids acting like kids.

A couple days ago at dinner, 5-year-old Herbie asked where we came from.

"We evolved from other animals," said my wife. "We came from the apes."

Deciding that the subject needed more clarification, I added: "You see, kids are monkeys until they're 3 years old. That's why they can't talk. They they learn how to talk and they turn into humans."

What I didn't say was that evolution is being reversed by video recorders. They are, in their own way, making monkeys out of all of us.

Pam gets married

"If I were a carpenter,
And you were a lady,
Would you marry me anyway,
Would you have my baby?"
Tim Hardin

The last of the great '60s women bites the dust.
My older sister, Pam, called to say she's getting married December 21 in Grand Targhee, Wyoming, and she wants us to be there.

You've probably known someone like her. You'd have bet the house she would never marry and then, boom, she's set the date.

I mean, there has been nothing traditional about this woman. In the late '60s, if you had a cause, she was leading it.

Pam was the first feminist I ever met. She was the first feminist ever to call me a chauvinist. Pam had a way of getting people to change, even if it's the last thing they wanted to do.

In fact, that's how we learned to cook. "Why should mom cook all your dinners for you?" she asked me and my three brothers one day. "What do you think she is? Your slave?"

Since we had didn't have a good response, we all started cooking dinners. I cooked cheese souffle for 42 straight weeks. That's how you get even with someone who calls you a chauvinist.

The first encounter session I ever went to was conducted by Pam in our family's living room. She thought we weren't communicating as a family, so we sat around leveling with one another. Or was that leveling one another? I haven't forgotten it, and I'll bet no one else has, either. Pam went to one of those experimental colleges that sprang up during the '60s. It was a school where you could major in making bread, a place where people drifted through and stayed for two months and became the president.

The college was in Vermont. I went to visit and Pam took me to one of her classes. It was held in a barn and the students were dressed as clowns. I thought, "This would be a pretty good college to transfer to."

I don't know how she came out of that school a photographer, but she did. And she's a pretty darn good one at that.

She didn't let her social life go, either. Pam always had plenty of boyfriends. They all had beards and were slightly built. As far as I could tell, they could have been brothers.

I remember one in particular. He had a light brown beard. He was thin and quiet. He was an only child with a penchant for academics.

He came to visit the family in Bakersfield for a week. You could tell he had never been around kids before. The second day, he disappeared. We found him in a dry culvert drinking a bottle of wine. Shortly after that, he went back East for good.

Finally, she met Cary. He was different from the rest. He didn't have a beard and he was stronger than a bull moose. No one thought the relationship would take hold, except the two of them. I wouldn't second-guess her, mostly because it wouldn't do any good. Pam's been her own woman from Day One.

She's headstrong, but there's more to her than that. She's always had a fierce desire to do the right, the responsible and the moral thing.

And she does it at her own pace, in her own way and on her own terms.

I love her for that. And respect goes without saying.

Pam's getting married with God, the family and a few deer as witnesses. If they have their way, you can count on three feet of snow and couscous for the wedding dinner.

It's a good match. He's a finish carpenter. And she's quite a lady.

Staying home

Wednesday is my day to stay home while my wife troops faithfully off to her part-time job. Instead of hiring baby sitters, I have a hand at managing a household that includes two small children. It has been a learning experience.

I am by no means the first among my friends to do this. Others have trod this path, but none so aptly as I. That's what every guy thinks. Fathers finding themselves in similar circumstances reduce the experience to two goals. Let me make it through the day. And boss, don't fire me when I'm gone.

Let's start with a few tips on child care.

RUN, CHASE OR DUNK THEM. The idea behind this is to get the children so tired that they sleep most of the afternoon.

GO TO MOM'S. Valuable time can be killed at a relative's house. There is also the possibility that grandmother will take her darlings off your hands for a couple of hours.

FARM ONE OUT WITH THE NEIGHBOR NEXT DOOR. Simple mathematics. If you have two, this leaves you with one.

ENGAGE THEM IN OUTDOOR PROJECTS. This strategy works if you have an inexhaustible supply of tools.

Wednesday actually starts on Tuesday night. Kids are bathed earlier and dishes done sooner. The count-down begins for my wife and me. There is tension in the air as we get ready to swap roles. My wife is happy and unhappy about leaving the kids. Again I marvel how my father managed to support the household and six kids with only one salary.

On Wednesday morning, etiquette is simple. Keep the kids out of the bathroom while my wife is putting on her makeup. If not, prepare to face the Wrath of Khan. Secondly, kiss her on the cheek after she has applied her lipstick. Thirdly, don't choose the moment before she leaves to tell her about the $100 I blew at the bike store Tuesday.

On this particular Wednesday, I felt pretty good. I got up, and took that early-morning pre-kid shower. My wife left without incident. Taped on the refrigerator was a long and detailed list of things to do.

I didn't panic, because the list could be called a husband's bible. I merely translate the list into two categories, long term and short term. I ignore the long-term items. They will return on next week's list. Also, this provides fodder for conversation in the coming week. They are the do-sometime-before-you-die-jobs. We accomplish the short-term.

It's 8:15 and time for the kids' breakfast. No bowls for cereal. Where are they hidden? The search ends in the fridge. The handsome little blue bowls hold last night's lemon chicken, whipped cream, and twice-around-the-block Chinese food. I make a mental note to ask my wife about this. I could pull some clean bowls out of the dishwasher but if I do so, I acknowledge the existence of clean dishes, which means that the racks must be emptied. Guilt by association. Emptying the dishwasher is not on the list, so I make other arrangements.

The first decision after breakfast is whether to pick up the Cheerios and bananas on the floor or just walk on them the rest of the day. Compromise. Clean a little path through the heavily traveled area but leave the scraps under the high chair and table.

Should I make the bed? It's an unwritten item on the list that may turn into an issue depending on what kind of day Sue has had. Every husband picks out one issue on which to take a stand. A last stab at masculinity. Some men stand for justice, others for truth, and still others for not making the bed. Today, I stand for not making the bed.

Since I didn't make the bed, I decide to make bran muffins. Every man who stands for something needs a counter issue with which to defend himself when the tomahawk comes winging his way. ("But I made muffins, honey.")

I lace on the apron. Today is the day for the TV repairman to come. I try to remember to take off my apron when the doorbell rings. I'll gladly make muffins, but the apron is my own little secret. I rehearse the conversation if the doorbell rings and I have forgotten to take off the apron. "Excuse me while I slip into something more comfortable," or "Don't mind the apron, I was just out shoeing my horse in the back yard."

It's time to take the older child to preschool. She cries and doesn't want me to leave her once we are there. I feel valued but sad. The teacher assures me that Katie does, in fact, have a good time at school. Nonetheless, it's hard to see my daughter cry.

Lunchtime. The little one is hungry. When he gets his fill of yogurt, he feeds me and is delighted each time I bite the spoon. When I ask him if he would like to take a nap, he laughs. All of a sudden, I love him very much.

My turn for lunch. The fridge is full of delicious leftovers. It's important to establish a policy on leftovers. I try to remember ours. Eat leftovers, and you risk devouring the family dinner. If you choose not to eat the leftovers and they turn out not to be tonight's dinner, some good-eating chicken and potatoes have gone to waste. If you eat tonight's dinner, try the following excuses: (1) You didn't expect me to eat leftovers for dinner. (2) There wasn't enough for dinner anyway. (3) We haven't had pizza for awhile.

The muffin pan was still in the sink. Twelve muffin cups, each with a mind of its own. She hates to do muffin holes. Causes headaches. I wash the muffin pan.

It's time to pick up the 3-year-old from preschool. I break into a full galloping sweat putting the little one into the car seat. He says, "Hot, hot," and I say I know it's hot.

We pull up to the preschool. It looks like a Volvo convention.

The kids are wiped out. The teacher hands me a duck (or chicken, bear, marmot - take your pick) made out of construction paper painted over with purple paint. We'll have to get a new refrigerator on which to put it, since the old one is plastered with ducks, chickens and varmints from previous classes.

I put the children in their car seats. I curse the technology of car seats. Putting kids in car seats is not only hard, it's undignified. Inside, you are fumbling with straps while your backside is halfway across the street. The person who designed car seats never put two or more kids in them in the Bakersfield summer heat. Next to aerobics, it's the best exercise you can get.

Halfway down 18th Street, the 3-year-old wails, "You forgot to strap me in." Usually, that would be cause for celebration but when she is tired, it becomes a major midafternoon crisis. I stop the car to do some more buckling. We drive home without further incident.

When we return home, I try the very delicate task of putting two kids down at the same time for naps. Degree of difficulty, 9.9. Chris Schenkel has called it the most difficult maneuver in America.

Everything has to be right. The phones can't ring, no one can knock on the door and holding my breath helps. Three hours later, the phones stop ringing. In the meantime, the TV gets fixed, dishes washed and the house cleaned. There are no naps, but why sleep when daddy is around? I relax a little bit. Why am I in such a hurry to get some unknown place and what will we do when we get there?

I stop and remember what it was like to be a child. We eat muffins and play in the sun.

The apples can wait

My father gave me a crisp $20 bill. I was supposed to use it to pay a baby sitter, but I didn't. I squirreled it away. I never know when I might need it.

Very early Friday morning I woke up with my pregnant wife tapping me on the shoulder. She whispered (so as not to wake our 4- and 2-year-old children), "I think it's coming," she said. "How many contractions?" I asked. "Three or four. I've already called your parents. They're on their way over," she replied.

A smart man could have seen this thing coming. It wasn't just that she was two days overdue. More telling was the fight we had earlier in the evening over whether we should do the dinner dishes or leave them until morning.

She didn't want my parents to face a sinkful of dishes if she went into labor. It's just the kind of thing you argue about before you have a baby.

My parents arrived a few minutes later. For the first time, they looked like grandparents - not old or anything, just seasoned.

The mood was light on the way to the hospital. We were joking a lot until she looked down and saw the red danger sign of an empty gas gauge. I told her not to worry since I had put a buck's worth in yesterday. She asked me why I hadn't bought some gas with the $20 that Dad had given me. I told her that you couldn't break a $20 to get gas.

At 22nd Street and Chester Avenue, she got a stricken look on her face. "Oh my gosh, I forgot to buy apples. The kids won't have anything to eat tomorrow," she said.

If this had been our first kid, I probably could have flipped a U-turn and headed for an all-night supermarket. A man would do some funny things if he went along with every single thing his wife said during labor. "Jump out the window." Sure, I'll do that. After a couple of babies, a husband begins to trust his instincts again.

What I did was to listen intently, keep on driving and wait for the next contraction. By 24th Street, we were through the apple crisis.

At the hospital, I grabbed the suitcase out of the back seat. I wasn't beyond help. Two babies ago, I had stared at it dumbly, thinking, well, it's her suitcase.

I teared up in the long hallway that connects the hospital lobby with the baby ward. The hallway seemed to represent one of life's transitions. We were leaving one life behind and another one was rushing in to take its place.

I looked down at my wife, who was being pushed in a wheelchair by the nurse. I put my hand on her shoulder. She looked up and smiled. Having a baby is one of the nicest things you'll ever do together.

I missed the old delivery room. We had requested, and gotten, the more homey Alternative Birthing Unit. The ABU with its relaxed, living room-like ambiance is a contrast to the openness and gleaming stainless steel of the more traditional delivery room. The delivery room had always seemed a place where technology and one of life's miracles come together in a deafening roar.

At 5:01 a.m., 31 minutes after entering the hospital, Samuel John Benham came quietly into this world. He weighed 7 pounds, 10 ounces, but I'm telling everyone he weighed 8 pounds. Eight pounds sounds more like a boy. He wasn't bad looking for a Benham; he even had a little hair.

Later I made a trip to the cashier's office. Ahead of me was a strapping blond man with an I-just-had-my-first-baby look on his face. We talked and compared notes. His wife had a 9-pound boy.

The cashier asked me how I wanted to pay for the portion that our insurance didn't cover. I gave her my best you-want-to-talk-about-money-at-a-time-like-this smile. Who brings their wallet to the hospital anyway? The cashier suggested the 60-day plan. How had I gotten out of there before?

I wasn't completely broke. There was a nice, crisp $20 bill tucked away in my shirt pocket. I was planning on using it to buy one of those colorful balloon bouquets for Sam's mother.

You'd have to agree that anyone who can do the dishes at midnight and then have a baby five hours later deserves one.

Ron May

The first time I met my neighbor, Ron May, I wanted to turn around to see what he was looking at behind me. He had fierce blue eyes and a way of looking through you that was unnerving.

Ron raised obstinacy to an art form. His opinions were deeply felt and barely hidden beneath the surface.

When we'd have our annual Halloween party, I would march across the street and ask him if he and his kids wanted to come.

"I'm not much for social gatherings," he'd say. "Kate and Beau can come but, to tell you the truth, there are some people in this neighborhood I can't stand."

At first, I wondered if he meant me. It took running up Rancheria Road with him on a foggy February morning before I knew differently.

Sometimes he'd shock me with his directness. People were drawn to him for that reason. He'd insult a person and make him or her laugh in the same sentence.

A while back, a new neighbor's son took a liking to Ron's daughter. It seemed a harmless flirtation, but it was Ron's only daughter and he didn't care for it.

He went across the street to talk to Jack, the boy's father.

"Your boy's taken a shine to my daughter and he's too old for her," he said. "I just want to tell you that I may have to kick his ass."

"If that's the way you feel, you may have to try his old man first," Jack said.

Ron laughed and from that moment they became good friends.

He loved his kids. When he saw our babies he'd say, "Kids are the best thing I've ever done. I'd have a dozen more if anyone could stand being married to me."

He grew even closer to his children when their mother died two years ago. On fall mornings, he and Beau would throw the football around in the street. He volunteered to chaperone Kate's drill team at Bakersfield High School. He was intensely interested in her friends and even took a few in when they were thrown out of their houses.

When the tests showed cancer earlier this spring and it was clear to him that he wasn't going to live to see 45, he started selling things. He had the only estate sale I've ever seen where the guy was still alive. He didn't care. He would have parked a hearse out front if it would have helped sales.

He wanted his children taken care of.

"The money is in a trust," he said. "The kids have a home. All I have left to do is pack."

The last time I saw him, I asked him if he was afraid.

"No," he said. "In Vietnam, I was

afraid." He left nothing to chance through his final instructions. In part it was a fierce protectiveness toward his children. But Ron also hated the idea of people messing in his business.

There was to be no death notice, no obituary and no party. He didn't even want people thinking about him.

He'd kill me if he knew I was writing this but he did give me permission to use him in a future novel. This is a warm-up.

On the day he died, a pine tree in the front of his house sagged and started to fall over. Ron hated that tree and would have been pleased to know that it might be dying.

On the same day, the desert tortoise eggs hatched in Ron's back yard. One by one they began marching out of the hole. That would have pleased him, too. He liked those old leathery-skinned turtles.

Last Sunday, I looked out the kitchen window to see Jack, Calleen and their kids armed with Hula Hoes, rakes and brooms cleaning up the flower beds in front of Ron's house. Ron might have grumbled but he would have probably appreciated this spontaneous act of friendship.

"We miss him," Calleen said. "We sleep with our window open and every morning we keep expecting to see Ron."

I know what she means. We do, too.

11

Love and a 2-year-old

You never think you'll love anything as much as you love a 2-year-old.

I know you're wondering if I'm crazy. Or if my 2-year-old hit me on the head with his popcorn push toy.

Let me clarify. I'm talking about kids just this side of the terrible twos. They've put their big toe in the water, but not their whole foot.

They still have baby faces, rosy cheeks and hair that will go just about anywhere.

They're pocket-sized, often stumpy. What's more, you can still rub your hand on their head for good luck.

They're sturdy. Knock them down and they're up like rebounding bowling pins.

Everything's new, but not as new as it was before. They are growing up. Soon they will be a factor in family dynamics. Already they smile through the prayer at dinner. Have you ever seen a 2-year-old swagger? And grin like a carved pumpkin? Heck, they'd wink if they knew how.

Do you get the drift? They're learning things. And guile may be one of them.

For example, a 2-year-old really knows how to spill his milk. He's spilled it all along but now he looks you straight in the eye and pours it over the table, chair and floor.

Then he palm-paints in it.

Funny, isn't it? Before you fall on the floor laughing, remember how much you love him. Even if you have to grit your teeth a little bit.

What saves a 2-year-old is that he has learned how to hug and wave goodbye. How to kiss, rub noses and do both at the same time.

A 2-year-old kisses with his eyes open and with an amused expression on his face as if to say, "Silly people, why are you slobbering on me?"

You can sense a growing independence.

A 2-year-old starts playing back with all the kids who have played with him as if he were a doll. He wrestles, runs and falls down stairs. He wanders down the sidewalk when you're not looking.

He starts enjoying his bath. Gets out when you turn your head, and runs naked through the house.

You spend half your time swearing you'll never have another baby. And the other half hoping you do. We have a 2-year-old. His name is Sam. He's a kick, as a lot of them are.

When I come home at night he is the first one to greet me. He puts his arms up in the air to be hugged. His face is all ridges, folds and smiles.

He is like a little planet, suspended there, vibrating with happiness. His face is full of light. It's wonderful.

Having a 2-year-old is being real lucky once in your life.

Guinea Pigs

When you select your guinea pig, do not pick the first pretty one you see. You should always examine a pet for good health before you purchase it. There is nothing more upsetting for a child than to have his new pet die shortly after he has taken the pet home and has become attached to it."

- Encyclopedia of Guinea Pigs

My mother bought a guinea pig for each of our three kids. Katie named hers Rosie, Herbie tagged his Brownie and Sam followed suit with Blackie.

They were cute, furry and fragile. Brownie died first. Scurvy. Five-year-old Herbie was crushed.

We buried him in front of the garage in a candlelight ceremony. There were no guinea pig hymns, so we said a short prayer.

A few days later we put Blackie and Rosie in the same cage. We were hoping for babies. We needed babies because a few months later Blackie died. This was perplexing because we had been supplementing his diet with fresh carrots, spinach and vitamin C.

It didn't help. One day we discovered Blackie on his side, ready to join Brownie, his long-lost brother. A month and a half later summer came. Rosie had two babies. On the advice of local guinea pig fancier Karla Jadwin, we put the drink of astronauts, Tang, in their water. They thrived or seemed to. We gave one of the black babies to a friend's daughter.

After a near-miss in a microwave, that guinea pig died. Then ours died. That left us with Rosie, a sweet, tan little creature belonging to Katie, her 7-year-old owner. Surely we would get the four years average life expectancy out of this one.

Well "surely" left town last week. One morning, Katie discovered Rosie dead in what she tearfully described as an "uncomfortable position." Katie spent part of a morning crying on her mother's lap, wondering what she could have done differently. Besides sending them to a sanitarium in Switzerland or installing an intercom system in their cages, we did everything.

We buried Rosie by the lemon tree. That made 3-year-old Sam happy because he had grown to love burying guinea pigs. This time we had no ceremony. We had run out of prayers.

Katie made a gravestone out of a piece of white pine. On it she penned the following words: "Rosie died on Dec. 26, 1989. Katie the keeper of Rosie loved her." She framed the words with camellias and carrots, with the tops still on them.

A few days ago I swept out the garage, threw out the trays that held the wood shavings and put the cages away underneath the work bench. I have to admit feeling a certain amount of sadness for those bright-eyed little creatures that will soon become a distant part of this family's memory.

It made me think of the kids. And it made me think of the decade that stretches out before us.

The children are little now, and as bright-eyed and innocent as those guinea pigs. They still believe fervently in the power of a stick of gum, a pecan party in the back yard and a good game of Chase and Capture.

When this decade ends, they will be teen-agers. They will believe in different things.

Right now, we're a team. In the morning when they pad into the kitchen and at night when they run to the door to see me come home. I'm not looking forward to the day when there are empty spaces on the bench.

I recently read a book called "The Education of Little Tree" by Forrest Carter. Set in the '30s, it is the story of a Cherokee boy named Little Tree who lives with his grandparents in the mountains. At the end of the book, his grandmother dies and leaves a note pinned upon her fanciest dress. It reads:

"Little Tree, I must go. Like you feel the trees, feel for us when you are listening. We will wait for you. Next time will be better. All is well." Grandma.

Profanity

Herbie came up to me with an innocent look on his face and asked about a new word that he'd heard. He said it had four letters and started with "S."

We all know the word in question. Herbie's always been curious about language. And frankly, I think he knew what the S-word meant and how to say it, but he wanted to hear his dad pronounce it out loud.

I rose out of my chair like a big-hooded cobra. My first reaction was alarm. Then I caught myself and decided to take the reasonable approach because Herbie is not yet 6.

He is in kindergarten. He still sucks his thumb when he gets tired, worried and during the "very, very scary story" at bedtime.

He is also learning in leaps and bounds. This includes vocabulary. Some of it is charming and some, not so charming.

"We don't use that kind of language at home, Herbie," I said. "I know your friends say those things on the playground and you may even have heard them in a movie but they're crude, show a lack of imagination and are just plain wrong."

He looked down and said nothing. He waited for his father to say something fatherly. Comforting.

"It's an automatic spanking if we hear you use that at home," I said, resorting to threats. "Now I want you to tell me where you heard it."

He didn't want to tell me, for which I sort of respect him. Kids will rat on their brothers and sisters 10 times a day for stuff they didn't do. But ask a 5-year-old to rat on a buddy on something legitimate and he will get very quiet, stare at the ground and study his shoelaces for the longest time.

"Who invented that word?" he asked, almost indignantly.

I told him I didn't know but that I thought it went back at least to the 18th century. Some words are very old, I said.

Old. That's what bothered me about this whole thing. I know it's not the end of the world but when your child uses profanity, it makes him seem old. Grown up.

I want to keep him small. Cute. Lovable.

All I'm asking is that he be moral, mathematical, creative and smart.

But crude? No. I've been there. It's overrated.

Am I dreaming? Probably. But I have a license to dream, since I have a 5-year-old.

I know this sounds a lot like the age-old sin of living through your children, but being a parent is sometimes a matter of trying to even the score. I want Herbie to make the kind of world I haven't.

That's a lot of responsibility to give a child. I try to slip it in as small doses between the stories, the play and the laughter. I don't know any other way. I'm a rookie myself.

In college, I read Franz Kafka's story, "Before the Law." It begins:

"Before the Law stands a door-keeper. To this doorkeeper there comes a man from the country and prays for admittance to the Law. But the door-keeper says that he cannot grant admittance at the moment."

The man from the country never gets in. The doorkeeper feels the conditions inside are more dangerous than the man can handle.

Parents are like that doorkeeper, shielding their children from the inner sanctum of adulthood. "You'll get hurt," we say. "It's not good for you," we drone. We say the word no a hundred times for every yes we let slip by.

It's easy when the path is narrow and the child is young. But soon the road widens to Grand Canyon-like proportions and voices get lost in the wind no matter how loud we yell.

Humor us parents. All we're asking for is perfection. For just a few short years.

The Barbershop

On Saturdays, we go for haircuts. For me, it is an opportunity to shore up childhood memories. For my boys, a chance to spin some.

It is a pleasant way to spend a Saturday morning.

We go to an old-fashioned barber shop, the kind that has been around forever, but may not always exist. It takes a huge investment to open a shop. Who can pay that kind of overhead with $6 haircuts?

One of the differences between a barber shop, and one of the newer hair emporiums is what the patron does with the haircut once he leaves the shop.

A barber shop assumes that you need a nice haircut for mowing the lawn. A beauty shop figures you're going out for dinner.

There's room for both, but at our stage of life, when we eat at home a lot, a $6 haircut will do just fine. At the Oak Street Barber Shop, it's just Zane, Woody and Hugh, three mirrors -with their much-younger looking Navy pictures hanging from them - dark out-of-style wood paneling, and a good supply of Sports Illustrated and horse magazines.

The worn leather chairs, where patrons wait their turns, are slightly cracked with some stuffing showing through.

Occasionally, somebody will stick their head in the door, calculate the wait, and then leave when they figure it is too long.

But that's rare..

Most customers breathe an almost discernible sigh of relief when they come in and see the three chairs occupied. It gives a man time to catch up on reading, smoke a cigarette and watch the barbers quietly go about their business.

There is pleasure in watching a good barber work.

Zane is the artist. Quieter than the others, he is given to stepping back, cocking his head and looking at his work. He attracts a lot of patrons with beards who eventually end up going to sleep in the chair.

Hugh, the tall one in the middle, is versatile. Kids or adults, beards or clean-shaven. Hugh puts a fresh towel around the neck of each customer. He uses the towel to rub the client's ears with when he's done cutting. I get the feeling some people come in just to get their ears rubbed.

The kids want Woody, a small and lively man with an ever-present grin. They are drawn to him because he can talk silly and because he is a magician.

He can make a piece of gum appear from behind a little boy's ear.

His constant chatter, tinged with laughter, adds to the feeling of peace and well-being in the shop.

Time stands still in a barbershop. You can almost feel your heart slowing down.

"When are you going to remodel this joint?" jokes one middle-aged man with a silver belt buckled across his relaxed middle.

"Heck, by the time we get around to remodeling we'll be gone," Zane says.

The other barbers nod, a few customers look up from their magazines with mild concern, and the kids chew their gum, taking no notice.

I guess it'll happen, but right now, the prospect seems far away.

Derek and Court

I haven't written much about my Bay area brothers, Derek and Courtney, for a good reason. I'm jealous. They are both taller, better looking and, most importantly, they have more hair on their heads than I do.

That's one of the first things we talk about. Hair. Who's losing it fastest.

On a visit to Northern California, I noticed that Derek, the tall, 31-year-old brother, was wearing a pompadour-like hairstyle.

"Derek, you're wearing a pompadour. You are trying to create some elevation on top so that you distract people into thinking that you have bushy hair," I remarked early in the conversation.

I can say this because I knew Derek when he was a little boy and his hair was as flat as Texas.

Courtney, on the other hand, was trying for the Bruce Willis look which on him was electrifying, but nevertheless did not mask its intent.

"You guys are both losing your hair," I said. "Look at me and see where I'm at because in three years, this is you."

"Not me. I'm going to use Rogaine," Derek said, dropping the name of the $50-a-month miracle cure that balding men have to use the rest of their lives, even when dead, so that their hair will not fall out.

"You ought to get some too," he said, looking over my head.

"It's too late," I said sadly.

"It's never too late," he said with a flash of anger.

Before going to the gym for a workout, Derek and I drove to a little establishment called Il Fornaio, a fancy bakery run by thin women wearing sweaters. There are no fat people in the Bay area. It's the combination of the exercise, the bran muffins and the exhilaration of a deal with a Japanese client that's just about to go through that keeps them thin.

We ate the bran muffins and drank the cafe au lait on the way to the health club. Not only did I feel healthy, but with the cafe au lait, I felt intelligent and cosmopolitan, as if I had learned a new language.

As Derek promised, the health club had everything. Rows and rows of the latest Nautilus machines, squash courts, an Olympic-length swimming pool, a sauna, a whirlpool bath, steam and cold pool. And of course, hundreds of people in very good shape.

I felt funny and decided that I'd rather be home where there are lots of fat people, biscuits and gravy, and a sky that I cannot see.

A Bay area workout takes at least two hours. The exercises, the whirlpool, sauna and steam take a half-hour each. And, if you have a brother like Derek, add an extra half-hour to adjust the old pompadour.

After the workout I felt tired, I felt rested, I felt deeply in love with myself.

Later that day, Derek let me use his car phone on the Bay Bridge. After a 2-1/2 hour workout and a 1-1/2 hour lunch, it was time to firm up our dinner plans with Courtney.

"Courtney, I'm calling you from Derek's car phone trying to act like I'm talking to a Japanese client, when what I really want to do is discuss dinner."

Later I found that in fact Courtney has a Japanese client. I don't know what the heck he does with him, but the important thing is that he has one.

On the car phone, I paused for effect, as if I was waiting for a response from my client. I felt very important.

That night we did some dinner business at an Italian restaurant. Three hours of laughter, three hours of fun, three hours of brotherhood.

I had forgotten how much I like my brothers, even with their pompadours. We find that we are growing old at about the same speed. Give or take a little Rogaine.

After this last trip, I finally understand why they live in Northern California. There's no underestimating the allure of a bran muffin, a workout and a Japanese client.

Sam and the handcuffs

The in-laws visited from Arizona and the first thing they wanted to do was go shopping for presents for the kids.

Katie got a T-shirt.

Herbie got a pad and some fancy pencils.

Baby Thomas got a mirror toy.

And 4-year-old Sam got his own pair of handcuffs.

"I just couldn't resist," Grandma Bev said, chortling mischievously. "It just seemed like Sam."

The handcuffs, orange plastic, came with two keys. Like the real thing, they had an adjustable setting for small or large hands.

Minutes after Sam and his grandmother got home with the handcuffs, which he pronounced "handtuffs," he asked me if I wanted to play jail. I was a tad distracted, having just lit the barbecue and trying to remain available to both the kids and their grandparents.

"Just for a minute, Sam," I replied, not wanting to be remembered as a complete drag.

"Put your hands behind your back," commanded Officer Sam.

I looked at this little shrimp and said, "No way." What kind of sucker did this kid think he had?

When he realized I wasn't going for that trick, he put the cuffs over my wrists in front of me, adjusted them snugly and locked me in.

I shouldn't say snug. I should say tight. It felt worse than putting my hands through a chain link fence. There are three stages that one goes through with handcuffs clamped on. The first is fun. Isn't this a novelty?

Then, panic rolls in. The thought raced through my head: What if I can't get them off? We'll have to make a phone call.

Finally, there's rage. Will somebody get these stinking handcuffs off me right now!

It takes about 15 seconds to go from stage one to stage three.

"Sam, get these things off me," I said, trying to remain cool. I couldn't use the keys because both my hands were occupied. Everybody else had left the room. It was up to Sam, and he was in no hurry.

"Sam, if you don't get these cuffs off me, I'm going to break them to bits," I said.

This was no idle threat. Last week, I had watched videos of the Power Team, a group of evangelical weightlifters, break out of police-issue handcuffs. If the Power Team could do it with steel, I could surely do it with this thin, no-account plastic.

"Uhhhhh," I grunted, straining mightily against the cuffs. "Here they go."

The room was filled with the sound of handcuffs not breaking. I had done an excellent job of imbedding the plastic edges still deeper into the sides of my wrist bones.

It was then that Sam felt pity for me and unsnapped the cuffs.

The next morning while fixing breakfast I heard Katie, 8, wailing from the living room.

"Sam won't let me out of the hand-cuffs like he promised," she bawled.

Having been in the same spot myself, I told her I'd help. I put the key in, turned it, and promptly broke it in half.

I went to the garage to get the pliers. After 10 minutes she was free. We were down to one key.

Sam was evening a few scores. Evidently no long-ago slight was forgotten.

Later that day, he locked up the grandmother who'd paid for the cuffs. I can't imagine what she had done, but there he was grinning like a monkey with Grandma handcuffed.

"I don't know where the key is," he said coyly.

I wasn't even in the handcuffs and I went to stage three. "What do you mean you don't know where the key is?" I asked as loudly as the Phantom of the Opera could sing. "You find that key."

He remembered. We unlocked a grateful grandmother.

That evening in the car, he locked himself in the handcuffs. We told him he'll just have to wait until we stopped and that we had no plans to stop for quite a while. It could be days. Don't think we weren't enjoying it. We were.

When we stopped, he was still whimpering. He had chained his feet together.

Grandmother left a couple days ago. The handcuffs are pretty tattered and are on their way out. Before she got in the car, he kissed her and said, "I really like those handcuffs. Do you think you could buy me another pair when you come next time?"

She laughed. We didn't. You don't suppose.

Sedona

I found myself driving through the Mojave Desert.

"Why are all these people waving at us?" I asked my wife. It was a peculiar kind of wave that ended with them pointing toward the luggage carrier on top of our car.

On Wednesday, we packed up the Volvo and the four kids. We were driving to my in-laws' house in Prescott, Ariz., for a family reunion. We bought the luggage carrier a couple of years ago, after having a suitcase fly off the top of our car on a crowded freeway in San Francisco. It looks dorky but works well.

"Maybe we should stop and check the carrier," Sue suggested.

I pulled over. The top of the carrier had flopped open and the baby back pack was hanging on for dear life. Fortunately, nothing had fallen out yet. The good news was that the bike rack and bicycle on the back were intact.

The carrier's latches were broken. I needed more rope to tie down the top, but I was ropeless. The closest thing I had were the extra-long strings from my tennis shoes.

Securing things this way didn't go over well with my wife but I assured her that, doubled up, the strings had the strength of bridge steel.

The string held, and seven hours later we pulled into Prescott. Sue's father had asked us not to park in the driveway and, just in case we had forgotten, an orange warning cone sat solidly in the middle of the driveway.

Now where did he get that? I've wanted one of those things, but I assumed there was a law against common people having one. Did my straight-laced father-in-law lift it from a construction site?

John and Bev, wearing robes, greeted us at the front door. They were happy to see us, and we happy to see them. I told John I had run over the orange cone and he laughed. There is a place in this world for idiot son-in-law humor.

Thursday was a lounge-around day, but Friday we planned an excursion to Sedona, famous for its 300-million-year-old red rock mountains and its mystical qualities. Friends tell me that Sedona is the site of a vortex, which is kind of the opposite of a black hole.

It also has more Indian stuff than you'll ever need. I'd like to have a nickel for every turquoise ring I saw.

One thing Sedona's not famous for is its Mexican food. We arrived just before lunchtime, and with our group now comprised of seven kids and five adults, we were raring to eat something, pardner.

I asked a lady in a fancy pottery shop where she would go if she was new to town.

She sent us off to a Mexican

restaurant, with a glint in her eye.

We did, and the bill was $110.

Holy cow. No criticism of Mexican food or anything, but one of its many charms is that it's cheap. You can do the kids for about $2 and the adults can sneak under the wire for around $6.95. The whole meal ought to be around $29.

There went my turquoise ring. I had enough cash for a slap bracelet.

As usual, the best part of the trip was free. We splashed around in the cold creek that flows through the town and visited the Chapel of the Holy Cross, a church built on a cliff on the outskirts of the town.

It was inspiring. It may just have been the Mexican food, but I could have sworn I felt the power of the vortex move through me.

Saturday, we planned a picnic to Jerome, a spectacular turn-of-the-century mining town that, like Prescott, sits at about 5,000 feet. I got up early and rode my bike the 35 miles to Jerome where the families were to meet me around lunch.

There is no better way to see country than on a slow-moving bike. The smells overwhelm. A crew was building a log cabin by the side of the road, and I nearly keeled over from the strong scent of the fresh wood.

Farther up the mountain, the smell of wind moving through sage and a pine forest washed over me.

The last time I was in Jerome, I had a double cappuccino and a humongous cinnamon roll at a quaint coffee shop on one of Jerome's two main streets.

I went there first, and doggone it if the red-haired waitress wasn't there who had helped me before. This time she was seated at one of six tables on the rough-hewn floor fawning over a man with long, dark hair.

He was an artist. His name was Ukha. No last name. I had a feeling he was the man who could explain the vortex to me.

Where did you get that earring?

I was sitting next to a man named Ukha in a fancy coffee house in Jerome, Ariz., wondering if Ukha was his legal name or whether it had been bestowed on him on the second day of a Tantric Yoga retreat.

I didn't bother introducing myself because when somebody tells you his name is Ukha, you don't want to tell them your name is Herb.

I had bicycled 35 miles up the hill to this old mining town and was awaiting my family and a picnic lunch. The last time we had been to Prescott to visit my in-laws, I had done the same ride and had a double cappuccino in the same coffee house, served by the same red-haired waitress who was now fawning over Ukha. She brought him a hot, steaming, exotic-looking drink. She stroked his long, black hair. She even played with the handsome silver earring that hung from his left ear. We should all have one name and so much affection bestowed on us.

I asked him what he did for work. He hesitated for about 15 seconds. I couldn't tell if he was about to say something really profound or if he had just taken too much acid in the '60s and the relay switch was down. "I'm an artist," he said slowly. "I do pastels."

I asked him how things were going. "I just finished a month-long exhibition in Scottsdale and people loved my work. They couldn't keep away from it," he said excitedly, making waving motions around him as if people had been swept across the floor by a giant magnet to his paintings.

"But I only sold one."

How do you eat if you only sell one painting? Without exactly calling him a freeloader, I asked him how he was getting by in Jerome.

"I'm staying with friends here," he said, and with that, the red-haired waitress stroked his cheek as if he were her son.

I had a feeling that Ukha had been staying with friends ever since the '60s had evaporated like a big lake in places like San Francisco and Berkeley, Boston and Madison, and fell as rain into smaller puddles like Santa Cruz, Taos and Jerome.

Give him credit. He had done what a lot of us had talked about doing, and he was still eating.

In the '60s, the search had been for the meaning of life, in the '70s the perfect relationship, in the '80s a perfect place to live, and now in the '90s he was searching for a means of survival so he wouldn't have to experience the economic free-fall that might land him on the streets.

Meanwhile, he had jettisoned his last name, collected a thousand stories and had a red-haired waitress who thought he was Leonardo da Vinci. I wished him luck and left.

25

You've got to be careful how you wish somebody luck. You don't want to sound like, "Well, I know your life's been miserable so far, but maybe because of this fortuitous meeting with me, your fortunes will improve and you'll get a job."

I walked across the street and sat on a park bench in front of a fudge shop. An older man with a cane and a tan Stetson walked up and sat down beside me. Although he didn't appear to be looking for conversation, I was, so I asked him where he was from.

"Mesa, Arizona," he said slowly.

I told him I had heard it was hot in Mesa. He seemed to corroborate that observation by nearly taking a bite out of the end of his cane.

"It gets about 110 to 115," he said.

"What do you do when it gets that hot?" I asked.

He stared up at the icy-blue Jerome sky. He looked down at his boots. Then he said, "Let it be."

Let it be. I did.

A Yugoslavian wedding

My cousin, Greg, "The South Bay Heartbreaker", got married. We drove to Southern California to rejoice with him. Rejoice, because a Yugoslavian wedding is something to get excited about.

Greg Popovich is a guy who has never forgotten how to laugh. This helps when you get married. This helps when you are married.

The big news at the church in Santa Monica was that the limo had driven off with the bride's shoes. The bride was falling apart in the bathroom surrounded by her attendants and Greg was standing outside with a smile on his face saying, "And I thought I knew that girl ..."

The day was saved by the bride's mother who had brought an extra pair of shoes. Where do you learn something like that? I'll tell you where. From a wedding consultant.

On the subject of shoes, I looked down at my brother Derek's shoes and realized he was wearing a pair of black slippers. Slippers? Derek, who lives in the Bay area, is so cool he wears slippers to weddings.

Next year everyone will be wearing slippers.

As usual, Courtney, my youngest brother, who also lives in the Bay area, was wearing a suit that cost at least three times as much as mine. I think his tie cost more than my suit.

The highlight of the wedding was the ring exchange. Neither the bride or the groom could wedge the ring on each other's ring finger. The wedding consultant had forgotten to tell them that fingers swell up like pork links when you get married.

That didn't stop them from trying to force those babies on, which makes the fingers even puffier. I could almost hear my cousin and his bride muttering, "I'll get that ring on there if I have to break your knuckle."

The reception was held at the California Yacht Club. The highlight was 75-year-old Aunt Bernice singing:

"Tiny bubbles
In the wine
Makes me feel happy,
Makes me feel fine."

Next she sang a Yugoslavian song, "Samo Nemoi Ti." An older woman sitting next to me started singing along softly. It felt like the old country.

The funniest story told at the wedding was Greg talking about getting ready for the wedding.

"I didn't get emotional until I was driving back from San Diego about a week ago and I got stuck in gridlock," he said.

"I came up to the Border Patrol checkpoint in San Clemente and suddenly it overwhelmed me. I started crying. I thought about how much I loved this girl and how lucky I was to be a part of such a supportive family.

There were a couple of tourists next to me with Minnesota plates. The woman turned to her husband and said, "Either that guy's got to get another job, stop driving in traffic or see a psychiatrist. Whatever it is, you can forget about moving to California."

There was a brunch the morning after the wedding at Greg's uncle's house in Redondo Beach. The bride couldn't make it. "Too many tiny bubbles," smiled Greg. Somehow he knew that being a good sport is a good way to start a marriage.

Yes, one by one they march down the aisle. The longer I'm married, the more pleasure I get in seeing others do the same.

I know what they are going to go through. And I know how it gets better.

Suckerdom

Katie, our 9-year-old, called from a friend's house. "You gotta come down fast," she said breathlessly.

"It's something with Thomas. He's learned how to walk."

"Darn it," my wife said with a grin. "He's supposed to do that for his parents. And, anyway, he can't grow up yet."

That's what comes with having four children. The baby takes his first few steps, and we're not even there.

Thomas turned 1 last week and, yes, we celebrated. In order to entertain his many fans, we bought him a new plastic table and four chairs. He also got a king-sized piece of banana cake and he did what every child does at that age, he washed his face with it and smeared it in his hair.

And we loved every moment. It was more fun than "Phantom of the Opera."

You think you're going to be less of a sucker with each child, but it doesn't happen. The first baby is wonderful, but the all-dayness and all-nightness is so exhausting that parents slumber through certain stages of development. Or wish some of it away. I remember wondering if our daughter was ever going to sleep through the night and whether we would join her.

After surviving a couple of children, I began to realize the stages are brief. A couple months, max. And the road never doubles back.

The plan is for Thomas to be our last, which partly explains our complete suckerdom. He's been photographed, videoed, written about and fussed over more than all the other children, because we want this experience to go on forever.

His two brothers and sister are nearly as bad as his parents. Herbie, 6, comes down in the morning, picks Thomas up, puts him in the big leather chair, spreads a quilt over him and watches "Sesame Street" with him. They are soulmates. Thomas' eyes light up when Herbie enters the room.

Bumped aside by the birth of younger brother, Sam, Herbie has found his place in the family again. To really even it out, we should have another baby for Sam, who sometimes feels left out, but geez, this could go on forever.

The decision to have four was not universally applauded because big families are not in vogue. People look at you funny, as if you are squandering some of the Earth's precious resources. Your parents think you're crazy and maybe they are right.

I mean, we should fix up the house. Take a vacation. Get on with our lives. Keep having kids and all that gets put off.

Maybe this is God's way of trying to tell me there is no vacation. And, as fast as we can fix up the house, some other part of it falls down.

We've eaten some great meals in the last year, drunk some fabulous champagne, even been to Cambria for a romantic windswept weekend. We've lived a little.

But having Thomas was the best thing we've done by far. You can have the rest.

That's when you realize your planning and your worrying about money, space and your personal freedom don't mean a darn thing. Yes, you are a total slave to your children, but as a friend of mine said, the payoff is worth it.

And with a baby, it's daily. I would pay a million dollars to listen to that kid laugh. He sucks in air when he laughs. Thomas laughs all the time because we can't get enough of it and we'll do anything, including jumping out from behind chairs, to set him off.

I give him a bath every morning. This doesn't sound like much, but it provides us both a peaceful foundation to start the day. He trusts me when I hold him in the water to wash the soap off. A baby's trust is unblinking, deep and abiding.

I know I'm starting to sound like a hopeless first-time parent, but there's more to tell. Thomas has a little piano in his room. When he sits down to plunk the keys, he raises his hands way up in the air, as if for dramatic effect, and then crashes them into the keys.

When he walked the first few times, he put his hands over his head as if to say, "Look, no hands." It's like a kid riding a bike with his hands off the handlebars.

You remember your last child like you remember your last day at the beach. The gulls are crying, the waves crash against the sand, the kids are silhouetted against the darkening blue sky. You drink it in for memory because you know it has to see you through the winter.

We're suckers because we like this baby thing. We can't make money, we're so-so dinner guests and neither of us is breaking any career records, but babies we can do.

It's been great. Did I already say that? That's OK, I'll say it again.

Having children is the best thing that's happened to our marriage. And although we could periodically kill each other for kid-related issues, such as who should walk the empty clothes hamper upstairs at 10:30 at night when it seems like you've done a thousand things already, we'd have 10 more, if we had the money, the courage and parents who wouldn't completely disown us.

I'm not a formally religious man but I believe in certain things and one of those has to do with children. A 1-year-old is the clearest evidence that men have souls. It shines out of their eyes.

You experience a moment of grace when a baby looks at you like that. It's sheer luck to have it day after day.

No regrets. I only hope all my friends and family are fortunate enough to have the same experience we did.

Because the only thing better than being a 1-year-old is having one.

Say you do

I got a letter from my first girlfriend. She's getting married in June. Shouldn't she have consulted me?

I know that if I was really mature I would shout my congratulations across the ocean to where she now lives. Write her a letter saying big, generous things. Call the airlines and get my ticket early.

But for now I'll hold on to the memories. I'll secretly dredge up faults that her fiance is sure to have. I'll bask in my superiority. And most of all, I'll feel sorry for myself.

We met the first week of college in Philadelphia. Each of us was trying to get used to the coed dorm we lived in, which wasn't as hard as it sounds.

Everybody was trying to meet as many people as possible, without violating one of the unwritten laws of coed life, "Never get involved with somebody on your floor." We were safe. She lived on the fourth floor and I on the second.

We were as different as two middle-class kids could be. She was a concert violinist from New York. Her parents, divorced, were both high-powered academics. She was in therapy and said I was one of the first people she had ever met who wasn't.

She had some pretty good stories about therapy. One time, in the midst of uncovering layer upon layer of juicy psychological material, she noticed that her shrink was being unusually quiet.

She got up off the couch to where she could see him. He had fallen asleep. "And I thought my problems were so interesting," she said.

Pam was a beautiful, beautiful girl with wild, curly brown hair and a wide open face. She was given to wearing loose T-shirts and purple high-top sneakers. Dressing up meant a wonderfully embroidered Mexican wedding blouse. It was then that one noticed the blueness of her eyes.

She used to drag me places. On five minutes' notice we'd board a train and go to New York. She knew where to find old-fashioned marzipan-filled chocolates. Where to get the best Italian food for under $5. The freshest bagels.

I remember walking with her on a pitch-black Cape Cod road in the middle of the night, in the middle of winter. Without the wind it was 10 degrees above zero. There was snow and ice on the ground. When I looked up, there were more stars in the heavens than I had ever seen. We almost froze to death on the way to experiencing a higher reality.

By the end of our sophomore year, we were drifting apart. She wanted to be a full-time musician so she quit school and moved to New York to study with a teacher. Her new boyfriends were all musicians.

Four years later, upon securing a position with the Belgium National

Orchestra, she moved to Europe. There, she met a charming Scotsman, the first violinist in the orchestra. The rest is history.

I'm going to buck up here pretty shortly. Put aside my dreams. Try to remember that this is 10 years later and there is no way back.

But it's not easy. First love leaves an indelible taste in your mouth. It's hard to get rid of.

I'm going to write the letter. Send my warmest feelings to both her and her future husband. I'll wish them lots of luck even though I can't make it to the wedding. I hope her fiance doesn't take offense when I end the letter with "Love, Herb." I don't mean it the way I used to. It's for both of them now. And for a good marriage in the years to come.

Shoe shine

Is there anything more relaxing than getting a shoe shine? It ranks right up there with a glass of cold milk and a rubdown after a steam bath.

Call it escape, but a shoe shine stand is one of the last male strongholds. Guys can still go there and feel like 15-year-olds.

Barbershops used to be like that, before they went unisex and stopped passing out bubble gum.

Now barbershops have turned into beauty salons. You have an even chance of sitting next to a girl. You can't even find a decent hunting magazine. Plus, haircuts ain't cheap anymore.

A shoe shine is one of the last great bargains. For $2.50 you get a shine and some easy conversation.

It starts with getting up and into the chair. The shoe shine man removes one of the metal foot rests so you can climb up without tripping. You are surrounded by the smell of good leather, plastic spray bottles and different polishes.

First, your shoes are cleaned with a lathery soap, applied briskly with a brush. Your shoes and feet let out a big sigh and surrender.

Now, it's almost time to start talking about sports.

I don't know why it is, but a guy in a shoe shine parlor knows more about who's going to win a particular game than any man alive. Maybe it's the week or so of sports pages scattered around the stand. Or maybe it just goes with the territory.

During the first application of polish, you find yourself venturing opinions on things that you have kept a tight rein on for a long time. Don't worry. You won't be the first guy to spill his guts on a shoeshine stand.

Ready for a surprise? The shine doesn't end after the first application. That's just to get 'em in the mood.

What happens next is part shoe shine and part Hollywood. This is why you gladly give the man an extra six bits.

With two hands, the shoe shine man picks up a towel. He looks at it with a combination of disdain and admiration. Before you know it he snaps it, not once, not twice, but three times.

Then he goes after your shoes with that towel, snapping it every so often. Pretty soon you've got a shine you can see yourself in.

The rest of the day you've got a little secret. The world can rattle your composure, take away your business, but it can't touch your shoe shine.

Goodbye, Mary Decker

We are training for the 1,500-meter race in the county track meet.

Did I say we? I mean Katie, my 9-year-old daughter, who has been perfectly unspoiled about each of the three track meets leading up to this one. These included the school race, the regionals and the city meet, where she finished third in one of the most exciting races in history.

While some parents might worry about the overly competitive aspect of racing, I'm not concerned about Katie's perspective. She's healthy. Her father is starting to flip out, though.

For instance, the other day I was walking along and Mary Decker just popped into my mind. Decker was the great track star who began her illustrious career at an early age. After daydreaming for a few minutes, I didn't know which one was Katie and which one was Mary Decker.

I told myself I'd never be the kind of athletic parent I had seen while growing up on the junior tennis circuit. Those parents weren't just overly interested, they were mental cases.

Take my friend Perry's father, for example. Attired in an expensive tweed coat- summer or winter - he would stand behind the fence swigging a suspicious-looking tonic bottle while he watched Perry play tennis. At the end of the match, he would deliver a stream of criticism which would have been OK had it made any sense.

Another father would skip any post-match conversation and just beat his daughters in the car after an unsuccessful tournament.

My plan was to be almost mystical about my children's involvement in sports. They could choose whatever activity they wanted. I would be the "O Wise One" in the background supporting them in a greater spiritual sense.

Things changed the first time I saw Katie running the mile. What a stride! Unlike her mother, who runs like a folding chair, or her father, who beats the ground like an 8.3 earthquake, Katie's stride was smooth and quiet. No doubt she was one of the finest athletes this town had ever produced, and she was only 9.

The city track meet was held at big, beautiful Memorial Stadium on the Bakersfield College campus. You talk about scary for kids.

Eighteen thousand people, 17,000 of whom came dressed as empty seats. A soft red track. Five hundred screaming track stars with their respective schools' names taped to their backs.

It was pretty heady stuff. Thank goodness I'm a pretty cool customer.

Katie's race was first, and an official herded 10 very cute 9-year-olds into a staging area away from the crowd and several hundred years away from where we were sitting.

"Did you know this race is only 3-1/2 laps around the stadium?" my wife whispered.

Three and a half? We had developed a four-lap strategy. A slow first lap, the medium-paced middle two laps and the kick in the final one.

Somebody had to tell Katie! "They're going to explain the race to the girls, aren't they?" I asked grimly. "Maybe you should go let Katie know the race isn't four laps."

The deed was done and minutes later the gun went off and the girls started. Just what you want on 1,500 meters, a dead sprint at the beginning. It can be a 10-mile race and kids will start out at 50 mph. There's something critical about that early lead.

That's OK. We had a strategy. "Let the rabbits go," I had patiently explained. "You'll catch them later on."

So what did she do? By lap two she was in the lead chasing the carrot. Bye-bye, strategy.

I wanted to talk to her as she ran in front of us. Plead with her. But I was in a sea of screaming people.

Didn't they have some kind of walkie-talkie system we could put in her ear? I was not above investing in a little hardware if that's what it took.

She held the lead all the way through the second lap. I found myself standing on the bench, blocking out the six rows behind me. Objectivity? Right. I was just trying to hold myself back from jumping on the track and running the last lap and a half with her.

By the end of lap three, after stopping for a few seconds to fight off a side-ache, she had a firm grip on third in one of the most magnificently gritty performances I had ever seen. Who cared about first or second? There was something more inherently noble about third anyway.

She rounded the last corner and had 200 yards to go. Suddenly, I got a sinking feeling in my stomach. Her medal was in jeopardy. A girl was coming up fast on her shoulder, and Katie clearly didn't see her. Even if she had, it was unclear whether she could have responded to her speed anyway.

With 15 yards to go, she caught Katie. Katie calmly looked the challenger in the eye and out-sprinted her at the end. My wife and I jumped into each other's arms and then ran out onto the field, knocking down a half-dozen signs that said, "No parents allowed."

We hugged Katie. I told her I was proud. I would have bought her a car at that moment if she had asked.

I said I wasn't going to get involved. I said I wasn't going to be one of those stage fathers who waits anxiously in the wings silently reciting every line. I said a lot of things.

I lied.

The county track meet is coming up, and I already have a plan. I need a stopwatch and a blue baseball hat with UCLA written across the bill. We're right on schedule.

Did I say we? I meant Katie is doing just fine.

Don't use the good scissors

Marriage.

It can be as real as a straight-edge razor scraping across your face or as ethereal as the fall wind blowing through your hair. One minute you're sweating bullets and the next, gushing poetry.

We've celebrated our 10th wedding anniversary. If I told you it has been easy, I'd be lying. But we made it, and for most of us who've gone this long, that alone is an accomplishment.

Things look different than they did 10 years ago. Things look different than they did two years ago.

Ten years ago we were going through the fire, but I am not sure what we were forging.

Now I think we're getting silver that one day may turn into gold.

But that's a ways off. We need a little more fire. A lot more metal.

Marriage is as much about lack of comfort as it is about comfort. The other day Sue called me at work. The conversation had something to do with the school candy apple sale. At the end of the call she asked me if I had seen her good scissors.

"I can't seem to find them."

I got that prickly feeling up my back. Yes, I had seen her good scissors. I even had the pleasure of using her good scissors in the bedroom renovation.

"They are in the bedroom," I replied, trying not to lose my poise. "I was using them to cut sandpaper."

The reply came like a knife. "Don't use my good scissors to cut sandpaper."

Marriage is getting that prickly feeling up your back when you start to do something with good intentions and things go sideways. What I was really trying to do was cut the sandpaper, so I could sand the trim, so I could paint the room, so she could spend the last few months of her pregnancy in clean, pleasant surroundings.

It takes almost 10 years to forgive each other for making those kinds of bonehead mistakes and 10 years to stop counting the times that you do.

The conversation ended with laughter. A few years ago it would have been silence.

A lot has happened. Three beautiful kids that I would die for. That I have died for, if anybody believed my periodic moaning about how tough it is to have children.

The experience of children is profound, joyous, exhausting and addicting. Sue is a terrific mother. There is a fierceness to her love that the kids never stop experiencing, whether they've been crab apples or angels. It's hard not to admire that quality. Impossible not to respect.

Marriage sneaks up on you in that way. One day you feel like bopping your spouse over the head with a 2-by-

4. The next, you want to gather her up and not let go.

It's absolutely the most confusing thing you'll ever do in your life. Only because you thought you knew this person before you got married. And more importantly, you thought you knew yourself.

You didn't, but stay married for any length of time and you will.

Ten years ago I wanted to conquer the world. All of it. Now I'm happy if I get the bedroom done before Christmas.

The conquering mentality is not the most useful attitude in a marriage anyway. Put on the helmet and expect the sword. Brandish a mace and get ready for a guided missile.

Last Thursday I called a flower shop to order a bouquet. Like most people I usually just call up and say, just do something nice. This time there were specific instructions.

"It's been work and I want something to reflect that," I said.

The florist laughed. He must have been a married man.

"I want something to reflect the joy as well as the pain," I explained.

"Well, we have something we call parallelism," he replied. "It's a European design. The arrangement has low flowers and tall flowers. I can't guarantee she'll get it, though."

In 10 years I have learned not to underestimate this woman's intelligence.

Parallelism couldn't be more appropriate.

In the early days, we crossed swords as often as we crossed paths. Now it looks like we're heading in the same direction.

Brotherly love and more

My brother, Derek, called to announce that he was a father. He was oh, so mellow. His voice has a special, "My- wife-just-had-an-8-pound-9-ounce-boy" tone of voice that seemed to drift high above the power lines. He didn't need a phone. Derek could have mailed that one in with his heart.

Derek is four years younger than me. His face as a boy - freckles surrounded by a mop of brown hair - was a cartoonist's delight. He could have been a character in a children's book.

Derek's a hard guy to stay mad at and I've been pretty mad at him through the years. As a child, before he grew tall and graceful, he was sluggish and TV-bound. He used to drive our folks crazy and I, as his older touch-football-playing brother, wasn't that wild about his fully developed sense of relaxation either.

Then he became active and obsessed with basketball. Derek was stubborn. He refused to back down in the one-on-one games we played, even though I had years and some height on him for a while.

He was also funny, sincere and when I went away to college, I missed him more than any of my other siblings. That kind of surprised me.

Derek was the world's most irritating college student. At least for his family.

He would throw Kierkegaard's name around like they shot baskets together. Nietzsche, he knew Nietzsche better than Nietzsche knew Nietzsche. He raised pomposity to an art form that approached Greek sculpture.

Of course I was perfect then, too, so I can say these things.

We ended up in the same business together, selling wine. We were on the same team, but at the same time we weren't on the same team. I liked the people I liked and he liked the people he liked and they weren't the same people.

Plus, he was good at what he did and I wasn't ready for that. Younger brothers aren't supposed to sell more wine than their older brothers.

After I left the winery we both worked for, he ended up running it. Younger had overcome older. And older was having trouble with it.

He married smart. His wife, Rachel, is beautiful, dynamic and somehow succeeding in doing what we all had failed to do: get him to stop talking like William F. Buckley. A few years ago we became friends again. I knew we were friends when we started talking and laughing late at night on the phone. Yes, it's hard to stay mad at Derek. Even when he's pulverizing you at almost every single thing in your life.

He makes a lot of money. He and Rachel have fun together. He's good to his mother and a valued companion to his father.

Now Derek and Rachel have a little boy. You should hear him talk about how proud he is of his wife and how pristine his boy is. He's like the biggest sucker on earth.

"I'm a father now," he said the other night. "I'm a father."

This has been one of the best and worst years of Derek and Rachel's lives. In October, they lost their house in the Oakland fire. Rebuilding has proved difficult for them, as well as for a lot of other people.

But the baby evens the score. The fire seems forgotten. There is a dark-haired boy to try to figure out and Derek is already trying.

Derek asked me for advice the other night. I was so shocked, I just about hung up on him.

"What do you do when he keeps crying and you've done everything?" he asked.

I couldn't help but feel a tad superior. I've been waiting for this moment for a long time. It's my one area of expertise. But shoot, give him time and he'll be giving me advice.

Derek being Derek is insisting on some perfectly annoying name, Zadoc. I told him not to think about it.

"Just let Rachel choose the first name," I said. "It's not that big a deal."

He took it gracefully. It was a new era. One that I had been looking forward to for a long time.

Sam and the Pilgrims

Sam woke up one recent morning and wanted his hair combed. It startled the whole family.

Combed hair? Sam, 5, owner of a longish blond crew cut, never wants his hair combed - much less somebody's hands anywhere near his face. "I think he's getting sensitive about his cowlicks," his mother conjectured.

What Sam was worried about had nothing to do with his cowlicks. It was the morning of the Franklin School kindergarten Thanksgiving program. Sam, who has this low gravelly voice, was one of the narrators.

His teacher had been almost as shocked as anyone when Sam, along with a classmate, A.J., raised his hand a couple weeks ago to volunteer for the part. Sam as the pilgrim narrator is like Bo Jackson playing Hamlet. He could do it but he'd have to do some cross-training.

Sam was a late talker. He is a physical child who already uses a tool belt. He has a pretty good left hook he hasn't used more than 10 times in the last year.

Third in the family, Sam is not normally the talent-show kind of child. His sister, Katie, will try out for any play, play any instrument and go out for any sport.

Herbie can sing and will. When he specializes in something, he knocks it down.

Twenty-month-old Thomas is just plain cute. He's the world's baby. Thomas is the friendship capital of the world.

Sam operates in their shadows and isn't always crazy about it.

Maybe it was his time to burst into the sunlight.

"Maybe he volunteered because no one else would and he felt sorry for Miss Hamby," Sue said.

Sympathy is not an integral part of Sam's personality. If he volunteered, it wasn't because he felt sorry for Miss Hamby. He may have done so because he felt chivalrous, or because he was in love with her or because he felt protective. But sympathetic, probably not.

Two days before the program Sam started having second thoughts. Even two-a-day workouts with his mother did little to quell his growing disenchantment.

The night before I asked Sam to recite his lines during our good-night cuddle.

"The pilgrims were happy to be in the new land called America. They enjoyed their freedom. We would like to sing 'America.' After we sing it one time, please stand and sing it with us."

He said it perfectly. He said it sheepishly. He said it like he might not say it again.

The morning of the program Sam

asked his mother if she ever got nervous before she talked. "Yes," she said. "Even Daddy sometimes gets nervous."

Nervous? I am the world's worst public speaker. Once I gave a 20-minute talk to a service club in five minutes.

Recently, a friend asked if I might be interested in emceeing a little event for 300 people. Sure. As long as 298 of them don't show up.

No, whatever public speaking ability Sam got, he got from his mother.

The cafeteria was packed with parents and the room resonated with the pre Thanksgiving heat of 200 anxious parents holding camcorders. First there was a stirring rendition of "Over the River and Through the Woods" and a song called "The Mayflower," where some clever children warbled about coming across the ocean on the Cauliflower. Then the audience got a near-perfect introduction to "Ten Little Indians" by one of Sam's female classmates.

After a very satisfying version of "Gobble, Gobble, Strut, Strut," it was Sam's turn. He got down from the risers and made the long steps up to the stage. A sixth-grader, holding the script and acting as the prompter, stood in between Sam and his classmate.

There appeared to be some commotion on the stage as Sam brushed away the script. Before the other child could get going, Sam put his face in front of the microphone, looked straight out into the audience and recited the speech word for word, booming it off the back wall.

Were we proud? Our heads were bigger than a pair of hot air balloons.

It was time to sing "America." Would we stand up and sing? You bet we would.

I felt as if I could go up on stage and sing it solo.

Halloween party

O ur haunted house on Cedar Street will be soon open for neighborhood business.

Last year, my wife and I designed our first haunted house. The 30 kids at the Halloween party agreed it was fine, but it just didn't stand their hair on end. They wanted more.

What did they mean by more?

The things I think are frightening, like crushing business debts and the thought of steamed broccoli three times a week for the rest of my life, are not haunted house material.

I needed outside consultants.

To find out what kids find scary, I called a colloquy in our back yard for eight neighborhood children ages 4 to 11. Some came because they wanted to find out what a colloquy was, and others for the lemonade and Willy Wonka's Wacky Wafers.

"Chris," I said, pointing to the Huck Finn-like gem of a boy who had the respect of every child, animal and parent in the neighborhood. "How would you like to be chairman of the haunted house?"

"Oh, neat," he said. "We can string a cable across the room and run a dummy dressed up in a gorilla suit. I've got this plastic head that you plug in and it moves. It looks alive. At the entrance, we can have a bowl of skinned cherry tomatoes for eyeballs."

With the mention of body parts, the rest of the group perked right up.

"We can use noodles for brains," said Aramee, an 11-year-old girl I hoped would consent to be Chris' assistant. "I think what we ought to do is lay out the slippery slide so people can slide into the haunted house."

I wanted to interrupt, but the group was picking up steam and this was no time to stymie anybody's creativity.

"Wait a second. Wait a second," said Herbie, my 4-year-old sidekick. "Do you know what we can do? We can draw pictures of Frankenstein and hang them up in the haunted house. That would be really scary."

The older kids gave him one of those "we'll let you stay because you're 4 and your old man's pouring the lemonade" looks, and then charged on.

"How about a skull with a small ax planted in it?" said 10-year-old Beau enthusiastically. "I've got some fake blood we can use."

"Ohhh," groaned the girls, shaking their heads and staring down into their lemonade cups.

They seemed to say, "Yes, these young pups really are going to grow up into animals."

Ten-year-old Janna suggested that we hang a black shredded sheet over the entrance for people to walk through.

"We ought to make a fake coffin and have somebody jump out of it," countered Chris. "We'd really scare people."

Forever, I thought.

One thing was clear. The boys wanted the real thing, and the girls the illusion. We compromised. We'd have a coffin, but nothing would jump out at you. The black sheet and the skull were in, but no ax.

For Herbie's sake, we'd hang up the drawings of Frankenstein.

In my next life, I don't want to come back as a human. I want to return as the patron saint of Halloween, a figure somewhere between the man upstairs and the skinny one below with the long fork.

It's not just because I love candy, although that's part of it. It's that the patron saint of Halloween gets to watch over kids' imaginations - a grand responsibility but terribly entertaining.

Timothy Rene Espinoza

Whisper to me in the night.
Wrap me in your warm pure light.
Teach me of the childish bliss.
Give me one more blowfish kiss.

Almost unnoticeable in last Friday's obituaries was mention of the passing of Timothy Rene Espinoza.

I say almost unnoticeable, because obituaries are as much a part of a newspaper's daily fare as the weather map, the baseball standings or the horoscope in our morning read.

We've grown used to them. We've come to accept them in a passive sort of way.

What makes this one different is the face pictured is that of a small boy. The obituaries are for older people. We know we are going to be in there some day, but that's later.

But little boys with big smiles? No. It runs against the grain.

His smile is infectious. That boy is on his way to a big belly laugh. And he looks as though he'd be real glad if he had company.

The face is full of joy. It looks flushed with the pleasure of being alive.

Espinoza is wearing a tie. He is cute. He is 5.

Several weeks ago, the class of 2000 started kindergarten. It was a class that had a ring to it. This class would make it. In a few years they'd be old enough to remember the 20th century and young enough to invigorate the 21st.

Not that they give a whit about this kind of thinking on the first day of school. Mostly, they were anxious to try out the stick of glue on their table. At recess, they were hoping to get a spot on the swings.

They are the peewees of the elementary school. All the other kids look big to them. The teacher's big enough to block out the sun.

Tim Espinoza, who died after a 5-month illness, was in my daughter's kindergarten class at Franklin School. They barely knew each other. The class was still in the getting-comfortable-with-being-in-school stage. It needed spaghetti feeds, art projects and field trips to cement things.

The obituary reads that Timothy Espinoza was a "loving, happy boy known for his blowfish kisses, his Big Bird blanket, as the 16th Street Air Hockey Champ and a fun camping buddy."

His father remembers him as someone who couldn't wait to turn 5 and go to school. His dad says that the thought of it probably pulled him through the summer. And for eight wonderful days, he got to take his new lunchbox to Miss Hamby's class.

He will be missed by those who love a really great smile.

His parents talk about being blessed,

and who wouldn't be?

He was special. He had to be. How many kids do you know who are really good at blowfish kisses?

Aim high, duck often

Lately, in my circle of friends, marriages have been biting the dust.

Five years went by without a peep of dissonance and within one week two sets of friends were throwing in the towel.

Maybe I'll get more mature as I see enough of this, but I was shocked. Saddened. The older I get, the more I realize that in relationships, the building blocks are not brick but sand. Beach sand. Fine, crumbly, subject-to-the-tides sand.

There is no way to feel good about the breakup of a friend's marriage. But, let's be honest, there is a feeling of momentary satisfaction - born out of the competitive spirit - that you have toughed it out and they haven't. It's a primeval, chest-beating, top-of-the-heap feeling, but it passes, swept away by the realization that the worlds we carefully construct are shimmery sand castles.

You get used to people being married. And sometimes there is as much comfort in knowing somebody else is going through the same misery you are, as there is going through that misery yourself. Not only misery, but near-misery, satisfaction, joy, love of children and years of watching the grass die together. Not to mention the fierce love that arises having done all those things together and lived to talk about it.

Marriage is akin to an artist slinging paint at a canvas 20 feet across the room. Sometimes he hits the window, sometimes the canvas and every so often, there is a miracle and a piece of artwork is created.

As a rule, the longer you sling paint, the better chance you have of making a miracle. The first few years, the paint mostly gets on each other. At that point, hitting the wall is progress. You don't even see the canvas until about year eight.

Marriage is about two different people, usually blockheads, who don't have the faintest idea what they are doing. There is no training manual for marriage. We all kind of blunder into relationships and then figure them out later.

Most of us start out in marriage dead-set on carving out our own space. "I did these things before I was married and I will do them now," we thunder. The thing that becomes clear is that space is not divisible by two. There is no house big enough, no marriage generous enough, no life easy enough to have all the space you need.

The next thing you worry about is your identity. Preserving it. This becomes increasingly important as you realize you didn't have much of one to begin with. Most of what we call identity has more to do with whether we opt for gin and tonic or a glass of cold white wine at cocktail hour.

So after giving up on this feeble space and identity thing, it is then time to get down to the business of marriage.

Marriage is an alliance. It's two elephants lumbering down the road, trunks swinging back and forth, heading for the same watering hole. Every so often, they stop and shoot blasts of cool air at the itchy spot behind one another's ears.

There is joy in the alliance. Shared purpose. A comrade in the trenches you smell the smoke with, the perfume, the flowers and the new grass.

Metaphors come easily in marriage but eventually it's about two people toughing it out. Which is exactly the advice I gave the last friend whose marriage was coming apart. He said OK, and hung in there a while longer.

The marriage got worse. Finally, they divorced in a sea of acrimony. He's remarried and is now deliriously happy.

So much for my wisdom. Nonetheless, it didn't stop me from giving my current divorcing friend a whole trailerful of advice a couple of weeks ago. This time I decided to stay away from specifics.

I talked about the end of winter. The beginning of spring. Light and darkness. A new dawn. It was more Willard Scott than Dr. Toni Grant.

After about a half-hour soliloquy under a moonless night, I put my head down and noticed him yawning. If he could have slept under the tree, he would have. The next time he gets divorced he'll leave town to do it.

Speaking for myself and, for that matter, to myself, I must say marriage gets pretty good after about 10 years. The one mistake you don't want to make is to tell people just how good it is because your relationship goes into an immediate two-week tailspin.

You learn to work together. The scars heal from the early days. You get a warm feeling inside. Love is not far away, but who's mentioning it.

Relationships are made of sand, but fine, clean sand. Add rooms, even a balcony to study the sea. Marvel as long as they stay up. Laugh if you can when they don't.

Watch the tides. Test the wind. Keep the faith.

And, when all else fails, thrust your hands in the sand and build again.

Did I really go to college?

M y wife asked me what we had to offer our kids and I was temporarily stumped.

It started a few weeks ago when Herbie, our 4-year-old, asked at dinner, "Do some people have dreams when they die?"

Think about it. Do you dream as you die? What a question. That's got to be the basis for at least two dozen religions.

I told him I didn't know the answer. I told him to eat his broccoli.

A couple days later, Katie, our 7-year-old, asked us to explain the meaning of the word "things." My wife sputtered for a couple minutes and then turned to me and said quietly, "Explain things to your daughter."

Things. Oh, that's easy, I explained. Things ... things. I started humming that song by the Statler Brothers that goes "Thinking about things, like a walk in the park, things, like a kiss in the dark" ... la la la.

That's as far as I got because it's almost impossible to explain things without using things to explain it. It's one of those words that evolved to the point where now it defines itself.

You either know it or you don't. You just hope that your children learn it the way you did. By feeling it.

Kids make you feel dense in a way you haven't in ages. At least since the Scholastic Aptitude Test in high school. I remember staring at that paper thinking I

was one of the dumbest guys in the world. And yup, I wasn't far from the truth.

Kids give you that old SAT feeling again.

A few days later, Herbie asked why we had to turn off the overhead light in the car when driving at night. This is a natural question because kids are always wanting the light on in the car and parents are forever saying no.

I told him because you can see the road better. Of course he asked why that was and I answered, "Contrast, Herbie, contrast."

Questions were multiplying like rabbits when somebody asked, "Why do you shiver when you get scared?" That one I'll welcome letters on because I blanked out.

I'm not a stupid guy, really. I can dress myself in the morning. Start my car, fix a fence and even change a faucet if it doesn't involve plumber's gunk.

But I don't know much about the way the world works, and my kids are discovering this. That may explain why when kids get to be teen-agers, they think their parents are the two dumbest people in the world.

Parents think it's just because the kid's gotten arrogant.

And the kid thinks it's because after 22,000 questions it's about time for an answer.

A few nights ago at dinner Katie asked why the musical scale only goes from A to G. Before I could answer, Herbie asked why you can't tickle yourself and make yourself laugh.

I went zero for two in two minutes. Send me back to the minors.

This brings back the question, what do we have to offer our children? I think I know the answer. It's that when you kids get smarter than us, we'll still love you.

Fishing

S pirits are never higher than before
a fishing trip. Dark thoughts are
banished to small corners.
Anything's possible, catchable and
bring-backable.

I planned to take the kids fishing in
a secret little pond off the bike path.
We would ride our bikes and fish for
the giant lunkers I knew were in that
pond. Between the four of us, I was
figuring 30, maybe 40, fish.

The last time we went fishing was at
a U-Catch-Em place on the central
coast. We caught 'em, but there comes
a time when you have to graduate to
the big leagues. Let the kids shed their
baby fat.

Before I go fishing, I like to load up
the backpack with at least 15 pounds of
stuff. The most important item is the
fishing pole that jabs me in the back
like a cattle prod for the whole bike
ride to the pond. Nearly as important
are the snacks - on this particular day I
packed Fig Newtons, apples and
crackers. Even though we were only
going for two hours, my kids will drop
dead if they are not fed every 45
minutes.

We caught the bike path at Beach
Park, turned east and headed to the
pond, about a mile and a half away.

After snapping the poles together, I
tied on a good old Panther Martin lure.
Fish love these lures. Can't stay away.

We scrambled down the hill and

positioned ourselves on the sloping
concrete ledge that fronts the 40-by-60-
foot pond. The ledge was packed with
fishermen grasping long, graceful poles.
One little kid on my right had a drop
line tied to a stick and was casting
rubber worms out by hand.

I took the pole first because I
believe it's important to establish a
certain tone for the fishing experience.
The fish tone. If you just give the pole
to the child and the child doesn't catch
anything, the child becomes frustrated
and may insist on eating and crying.

First cast.

"Daddy, are you supposed to
thrown the bait over the fence?" asked
7-year-old Katie, pointing to the metal
fence running along the top of the
pond that I had tossed the lure over.

Too much power. Us muscular guys
have that problem. Just back off a little
bit.

I did. This time I buried it in the
fence.

"When are we going to get to fish?"
asked Herbie.

My mood turned dark. "When I get
this lousy lure into the water," I thought
to myself. But I spoke civilly to my son.

"Let me just hook one up for you
and I'll let you reel it in," I replied
evenly.

"I caught a fish," said the small boy
to my right with the drop line and the
stick. Sure enough, a little sunfish

wiggled on the end of his line.

"That's the eighth one today," he said proudly, showing the fish to the children.

I cast again. This time the pole came apart and the top two sections flew into the water. The other fishermen gave me that "Go home" look. The kids looked puzzled.

"Do you want me to go out and get it?" the kindly voice of young boy with eight fish piped up.

"Yes, that would be very nice," I said. The boy waded out and retrieved my pole. I'm surprised a fish didn't swim into his pocket.

"A big fish," yelled someone down at the end of the concrete ledge. Yes, sure enough, an older man was reeling in a big bass that must have been two pounds.

"Let's go see him, Sam," I said, picking him up and starting to run toward the fisherman who now had the fish in his net.

Ten feet from the fisherman I slipped, fell and dunked Sam in the water.

"Daddy, you got me wet," he cried, looking hopelessly at his clothes dripping with smelly swamp water.

"Sam, it's only your shoes and pants that are wet. They'll dry off," I explained.

Sam was not convinced. Sam was not consoled. Sam was not my friend anymore.

Back at our spot, I handed the pole to Katie and told her to fish. She did. After a few casts, she caught a little one. She turned and smiled at me. How could you be mad at a little girl with a smile like that?

We got back on the bike path and rode home from our secret fishing hole. Sam was dry, Herbie dusty and Katie flush with her victory over the fish.

It reminded me of that scene in "American Graffiti" where Toad's date tells him after a wild evening, "I got to see you get beat up. I watched you get sick. Your car got stolen. What a night. I had fun."

So had we. Spirits were high. Dark thoughts still banished to small, dusty corners.

Boys' weekend out

My father, three brothers and I had a guys' weekend. We went to my parents' place at Mammoth and moved in with mountain bikes, running shoes and one bottle of Princess Marcella Borghese Clarifying Cleansing Creme.

You might wonder about the Princess Marcella Borghese Clarifying Cleansing Creme.

"Courtney, what is this?" I asked, picking up the handsome little apricot-colored plastic vial.

Courtney is the youngest and most handsome of my brothers, and if anybody could make a case for applying moisturizing cream to his face, he could.

"I didn't buy that," he replied somewhat defensively, as if its status as a gift justified his using it.

"You know how much this stuff cost?" he asked, shifting from defense to offense. "Thirty bucks."

Are you a damn fool? What's gotten into you, boy?

This exchange took place as he was getting out of the shower and I was getting into it. It was then I noticed the bottle of Body and Soul Apricot Cocoa Butter Lotion.

"I didn't buy that either," he said, after I had picked up the bottle.

Cocoa butter's great. You can either rub it on your arm or pour it over ice cream.

The boys' weekend out was my father's idea. A couple years ago God just about punched his ticket. The assumption that "we'll get together someday" seemed less a given than it had before, so we decided to gather now rather than later.

The boys went for the idea immediately. It was the women who needed a little persuasion. The natural response from various and sundry wives was, "Why can't we come?"

I'll tell you why.

Because we thought of it first. We thought of it first because as men, we are naturally more selfish. We'll try it and let you know how it works.

That Friday night we went out to dinner. We bought wine and soon we were toasting waitresses, the manager and customers. After dinner Derek, my next youngest brother, suggested that we go upstairs to the dance floor and do the chicken giggle.

The chicken giggle? Without our wives? Preposterous.

Actually, it was interesting to see who was going to break down and call his wife first. Saturday afternoon, after a day of trail running, hiking and mountain biking, Mark, the oldest and ostensibly the most mature, called Susan. It might have been sheer guilt over the great time he was having. I don't know what his excuse was, but he had one, and it seemed carefully rehearsed.

Afterward, the three younger brothers sat in the Jacuzzi scoffing at him and swearing that they would never call their wives. By Sunday, everybody had called home. Some twice.

You could tell people were calling home when they started whispering. I waited till everybody was in town buying muffins before I made my call home. That way I didn't have to whisper.

The two days were wonderful. We laughed so hard we could cry. I felt 12 again. We played and got along better than we had our whole lives.

It was a short intense window of happiness bathed in the brilliant fall light. But these things don't last forever, do they?

Sunday at 1:15 p.m., Derek got a call from his brother-in-law, Joe, who lives with Derek and his wife in the Oakland hills. Joe was hysterical.

"There is a huge fire in the hills," he said. "You have to come home now."

Derek explained that he was five hours away and tried to reason with him. No good. Derek got on the phone with his wife, Rachel, who is seven months pregnant. He instructed her to get the cats, the photographs, her jewelry, his files, the computer box, the business software, the art collection and his Italian suits.

She also had the presence of mind - and what I would like to think was an act of spontaneous love - to get Derek's ties. Joe and Rachel packed the cars and fled.

Half an hour later Derek and Courtney were giving us hugs, leaving the condo at Mammoth and driving back to the Bay area.

Rachel and Joe made it out. Some people went to the Red Cross shelter. Rachel and Joe went to their health club. Derek and Courtney made it safely back to the Bay area and there was a tearful reunion at Rachel's folks' house.

Monday afternoon, Derek and Courtney finally got permission to go back into the Oakland hills. Derek described it as resembling Dresden after the bombing. The pine and eucalyptus forest was gone. Their neighborhood was gone. Their house was gone. Nothing was left in the garage except the steering wheel of Joe's Jetta.

In the rubble, Derek found two things: a single ceramic cup that my mother had thrown on her potter's wheel and a page, singed around the edges, from a book on Jewish history from their college days at Berkeley. Derek and Rachel had met for the first time in that class.

Lois Sidenberg

M y grandmother in Santa Barbara is 89, but don't let her age fool you. Anybody who thinks she's ready to lie down is crazy.

It's not a matter of being spunky - that's too tame a word. Spunky is an attractive quality in other grandmothers but doesn't fit this one-time United World Federalist (political theme: "World Peace Through World Law") who took her first flying lesson in 1919 (she still gives airline pilots advice on how to fly) and claims to have taught Ethel Kennedy how to fox hunt.

No, her Jack Russell terriers are spunky. Lois Sidenberg has an acid wit, an unnerving recall and has absolutely no patience with the nouveau riche who have moved into her neighborhoods.

A while back it was Sylvester Stallone, to whom she was introduced at a party and didn't recognize. "Who was that awful man?" she asked unabashedly, after Stallone had walked away. "That was the movie star Sylvester Stallone," her companion whispered in awe.

"Never heard of him," she snapped. Stallone - who was later told the story - got a big laugh about it, according to one of grandmother's friends.

Grandmother doesn't have time for such nonsense. She's always been too busy saving the world from her canopy-covered bed with a bedside table overflowing with projects. If you find yourself on the other side of an issue from Grandmother, prepare for a blizzard of letters, position papers and petitions. Disagree with her in person and beware of the look - a combination of incredulity that you could hold such a stupid position, surprise that you haven't done your homework and sympathy that you weren't born with a little more sense.

If Grandmother has a weakness, it's her terriers. Generations have scampered through the house. Lulu and Rocky live with her now.

A couple years ago, a red-tailed hawk swooped down and carried off Arthur, an earlier representative of the breed, and dropped him unceremoniously from the sky. Grandmother responded by arming her house with rubber owls and snakes in hopes of scaring off the hawks. She also bought another Jack Russell.

A month ago, a hawk swooped again and picked up Rocky. Fortunately, the hawk dropped him on the way up and, miraculously, he survived. Now, Grandmother is a conservationist, but if one more hawk tries to make off with her dogs...

If the hawks weren't enough, our 3-year-old son, Sam, kicked Lulu right in the rib cage. We had one of those tense, freeze-frame moments that you hope passes before everyone melts.

"Apologize," she ordered the little man. "No," he said firmly. "Me no like dog." Sam, like his great-grandmother, doesn't back down easily.

No visit to Santa Barbara is complete without a Sunday outing to the polo grounds to watch a couple of chukkers of polo.

"Maybe you'll see somebody famous," Renata, the housekeeper, said at breakfast. "Last week Kareem Abdul Jabbar was there, and Stallone owns a condo on the grounds."

Grandmother drove her own car to the polo grounds. She was denied her usual parking place in front of the grandstands and had to park in the overflow parking across the rather large field. Feeling that the walk was a little more than an 89-year-old woman could handle, she drove across the field, scattering the two teams who were warming up at one end.

Sitting in grandmother's box, I turned around to check out the crowd. About eight feet behind us and to the left, Stallone was sitting with a beautiful auburn-haired woman who looked young enough to be his daughter. Stallone was wearing a tan fedora and was smoking a huge Cuban cigar.

I realized one thing looking at Stallone. There's a reason these people are on screen. They're handsome, I'm not. They can act, I can't.

Stallone looked happy, prosperous and Santa Barbara-y.

After a couple of chukkers, 7-1/2 minute periods - we got up to go back to Bakersfield. We kissed Grandmother on the cheek, everyone except Sam who doesn't have any use for that nonsense, and said good-bye. Grandmother walked back to her seat and began cheering.

Six grand and counting

For years, I've been seeing guys wearing gold Rolexes. Encrusted with diamonds and sparkling like the king's jewels. Boy, they get my attention.

You know how it is when you see one. You want one, you don't want one. You want to look, you don't want to look.

Anyway, this story begins when my second-youngest brother decided to get married. A San Francisco wedding. Big plush affair at the Mark Hopkins Hotel.

I couldn't just go. I had to be outfitted. It was one of those weddings that required an investment.

People worried for months about what they were going to wear. There were trips to Los Angeles. Clothes arrived by the bundle in the mail. Decisions were made and remade three or four times.

All for a guy who had been running around in basketball sweats his whole life. That is before he moved to San Francisco and got uppity.

A week before the wedding I went out to the tux shop to get fitted. I could have rented the burnt-orange one but this was my brother's coming-out party amongst the San Francisco hoity-toity and I really couldn't do that to him, even if he did drive me crazy at times.

I picked out a beautiful gray tux with razor-thin pinstripes. It was an uncriticizable unit.

After getting the no-slip shoes and the curiously named cummerbund (sounds like something to eat as in "put it on a cummerbund with all the trimmings"), I was ready to check out. The nattily attired owner was writing me up when I noticed a shimmering Rolex on his left wrist. "Nice watch," I said, wondering out loud how a guy with a small business could afford one.

"Like it? Check these out." He reached under the counter and pulled out a rich-looking jewel case covered with red felt. He placed the case carefully on the counter and opened it. "What do you think of these babies?" he asked.

I almost gasped. Inside were a dozen gold Rolexes, three or four Piagets and a couple of other watches with real small numerals on their dials.

"Look real don't they? You or me couldn't tell the difference. Especially from a distance.

"I can put you in a 'Rolex' for $200. Any of these other ones for $150. Try one on."

I reached for the Rolly and slipped it on. It looked like something from a shipwreck that had shimmered on the ocean floor for 100 years, the sea weaving beautiful patterns in the sand around it. I closed my eyes. I felt rich.

I tinkered with the idea for a minute. I could impress a few people at the wedding. My brother would faint.

He'd think, man, this guy's really making it.

I put it back in the case. Not because I was worried about wearing fake jewelry. It's just that the '80s are coming to a close. And the '90s will bring something new.

Something cheaper. Nicer, but more graceful. Something closer to where I want to end up.

Pregnant

The last few months of pregnancy are not much fun for anyone. The mother is gaining weight and, no matter what anybody tells her, straining to tie one's shoes is not good for the old self-esteem.

When you add awkwardness, exhaustion and a husband who never seems to do enough, you get a taste of what it's like.

A man's reaction is, "who is this crazy woman I'm married to?" Even-tempered women get mad for no reason. As they approach the witching hour, they do bizarre things in the middle of the night. A friend's wife painted her toenails before she went to the hospital. Some take baths, shave their legs or, as in my wife's case, fold laundry.

A baby on the way is no easier on brothers and sisters. Yes, there is tremendous excitement, but there is also a sneaking suspicion that things will never be the same again. Kids are seldom needier than a few days before a baby is born.

For couples, the final weeks before a baby arrives may not be the best of times. Both want the pregnancy to be over, but for nearly opposite reasons. The woman wants her baby. The man wants his wife back. What they want together is for their world to return to normal.

And it will, because babies rarely disappoint. Their births can chase away even the most frigid nuclear winter.

But before that sweetness dawns, you worry. About the child, certainly, but also the smaller things. Women worry about getting the baby's room ready, the changing table stocked with diapers, receiving blankets and sleepers. They check and recheck the hospital bag.

In our case, Sue made darn sure that the floors were swept and mopped at all times and made me promise not to wear my stupid white pants to the hospital.

I could only think about the car. We were having a fourth kid? What about the luggage on our next vacation? We couldn't use the back of the Volvo anymore, because the kids would be sitting there. Maybe we could tie the kids to the top of the car and put the luggage inside.

Labor started early Friday at 1:03 a.m. Five-year-old Herbie had come in and given his mother a kiss a few minutes earlier. A messenger? I don't know. But if so, the message was that labor, a monumental effort, is also an act of love.

Driving to the hospital was exciting. Things were moving quickly in the seat next to me so I kicked it up to 60 mph. It was sweet to accelerate past a police car and know that it didn't matter. He must have known. He just let us fly.

Parking and grabbing the suitcases in one motion, we ran to the hospital's front entrance. It was locked. Locked! Yes, the front entrance is locked after 9:30 p.m. Right then, in front of the fountain people throw money into, Sue had a screaming contraction you could hear in the parking lot of the Kmart across the street. We went around to the emergency room entrance.

That was fitting. My, now this was an emergency.

He was born 35 minutes later.

Thomas George, an early American. For a minute I thought we had the wrong kid because this one was not a conehead straight out of the chute like his siblings. He was good-looking from the get-go.

A baby doesn't change everything. We've still got luggage problems. The kitchen floor is dirty again.

But winter is over. That's what babies do. They remind you that spring is always waiting in the wings.

Sam's first day in kindergarten

S am told us he didn't want to go to kindergarten.

We were eating dinner, having a pleasant conversation about the first day of school when Sam asked what would happen if he didn't go to school.

"Daddy and Mommy might go to jail," his mother said, taking what we both knew to be a calculated gamble.

This is a gamble because Sam is not one to be bluffed. Threaten to spank him if he strong-arms his baby brother and he will thrust out his lower lip and say, "I don't care."

He is fierce about standing up for his principles. Sam is the Boris Yeltsin of our house.

He will be the first one of our kids to smoke a cigar, move into his own apartment and drive a Mustang convertible. A tattoo is not out of the question. I can see Sam in the Navy, standing dockside with the wind ruffling his blond hair.

"What do they give you to eat in jail?" he asked.

Sam is not stupid. If his parents had to go to jail so that he could stay out of kindergarten, so be it. On the other hand, if the food sounded interesting, then this might be a place he would want to visit himself someday.

Food is important to Sam, and to him a few nights in the slammer for food he liked would not be a bad trade-off.

A few weeks ago, Sam spent the night with friends. The phone rang at 11 p.m. and it was Sam, sobbing.

"I'm hungry and I want to come home," he whispered.

He was asked if there were any conditions under which he would consider staying.

"If they give me something to eat then I might stay, " he sniffled.

They did and Sam, 5, slept like a baby.

"I think they feed you a lot of beans and rice and meat loaf in jail," his mother said to the question on prison rations.

End of discussion. Sam's parents were going to jail without him.

Two days later, Sam and his mother went to visit his teacher and classroom. Sue volunteered to bring a plate of cookies for the pre-kindergarten reception. Sam had a proprietary interest in those cookies and he burst into tears when people began eating them.

His spirits improved on the way home when they checked the menu for the first week of school and he noticed corn dogs on Monday.

Still, he was not ready, and no form of bribery, either practical or frivolous, seemed to have any effect. I guess it goes to show that even a big independent guy like Sam - all 3-1/2 feet of him - shivers at the thought of putting a backpack on his back, a lunch pail in his hand and going off to square up with the world.

By Monday, the first day of school, Sam was ready. His mother had bought him one of those Igloo lunch boxes. Just in case she was grilled by the police, Sue didn't want to be accused of starvation tactics.

Appropriately, afternoon kindergarten starts out with lunch. After downing an egg salad sandwich, a pint of chocolate milk, apple, pretzels and a brownie, Sam hung his name tag around his neck and got in line.

Seated at his desk, he called for both of us to come and give him a hug. With his half-brave smile, he saw us out the door.

As I left, I turned around for one more look. Sam's head was bowed and tears ran down his nut-brown cheeks.

He took a deep breath and wiped his eyes with the back of his hand. Then he turned up his head defiantly, as if to say, "Ah, that's for babies."

Perfect baby

My sister was in town. I'm glad she came. But that baby of hers has me worried.

Alexandra Benham Simonsen is 5 months old. From handsome parents, Annie, as she is called, combines the sunshine of California with the rosy complexion of Norway. She is cute at an age when most babies are not.

Annie has a big, round face. North Sea blue eyes. And a mouth that's always smiling.

She sleeps from 8 at night to 8 in the morning. Annie eats every four hours. She rarely cries.

At the moment of her christening, held high above the crowd, she let go a big smile to everyone in the room. She doesn't even cry on airplanes. Annie likes her naps.

Now you see why I'm just a little bit worried. The baby's perfect.

Every family has one. The only problem is it's rarely yours.

How does it happen? Some people think it's dumb luck. Genes. Others owe it to how you bring them up.

For a moment, let's assume it's in how you bring them up. There are two schools of raising kids. Schedule them. · Or let them run the show.

Annie is from the first group. She was put on a schedule right away. At first, it wasn't easy. But after a couple of weeks, Annie and her parents got used to it.

Now everyone likes this predictable schedule. The baby likes it because that's all she knows. My sister likes it because it makes parenting easier than advertised.

Babies from the "run the show" group are different. They rarely are perfect. They have a tendency to nurse every 15 minutes. Wake up at 1 and 3 in the morning. Sleep like a rock between 7 and 10 a.m.

They cry during dinner. Or when you're falling asleep. They spit up on your wife's new dress just before you're going out to dinner.

When they get older they get up and watch the 11 o'clock movie with you. Crawl into your bed. Look you straight in the eye while they splash half the water out of their bath.

The run-the-show parents have their reasons. They have a cadre of experts to support them. A shelf full of books. If all else fails, they'll mumble something about developing creativity in a democratic environment.

They'll try to tell you that they like getting up at 3 in the morning. That king-size beds were made for five people. Tell you that kids under 2 should experience Belgian waffles at least once a week.

It's easy to pick out the loosey-goosey parents. They look like they have just come back from boot camp. They are strong but distant. The look in their eyes is not one of disinterest. It is from 20-hour days in the name of love. So I'm kind of glad my sister had to go back to where she lives. It'll give that baby some time to grow up. And learn a few things.

Just boys

My wife and 7-year-old daughter went to visit friends in Houston. That left the boys - Herbie, 5, Sam, 3, and me to do anything we wanted for five days.

Five whole days. Just the boys. A team grateful for the opportunity to distinguish itself.

Two hours after we dropped them off at the airport, Sam asked me where Mommy was.

"Houston," I replied, wondering about the little man's team spirit.

"Why?" he asked.

"To visit friends," I responded briefly.

"I want my Mommy home," he said.

I thought that kid liked me. Forget this team stuff. I had a free agent with no place to move him.

Thursday night I fixed carrot sticks and thawed out a pizza that I had bought from the symphony fund-raiser. Herbie ate his dinner because I threatened him and Sam didn't eat because I threatened him.

During breakfast Friday, Sam drowned his scrambled eggs in milk. I was not amused. Sam was on the trading block.

When I got the kids taken care of, I started thinking about the big plans I had.

Put up ceiling fans in every room in the house. Tear out the snow peas. Build a new fence. This place was going to look good. Sue would be impressed when she came home.

Heck, you're lucky if you get the table cleared when you're in charge of the kids. The dishes washed. The kids' room picked up before keeling over in exhaustion.

What I needed was a strategy. I decided on containment. Keep the kids alive and the kitchen clean.

Friday night the boys went to spend the night at a friend's house. I was alone. I had a beer. I ate a plate of spaghetti in front of a Lakers' game. I read a good chunk of a 300-page book.

It was wonderful.

Saturday, I started hearing voices. When I woke up, the voice said, "Make the bed please." After my shower it intoned, "Hang up your towel." When I finished breakfast it artfully suggested, "The kitchen floor really could use a good sweep."

That darned woman. Did she have a microde surgically implanted in my brain?

Sunday, the boys and I started getting along better. Containment wasn't working so I let them run wild. We started having fun.

Sunday night I started thinking about cleaning the house for the girls' arrival Monday.

It's not that you're trying to build up any points; it's that you don't want to lose any.

Vacuuming the rug is one way to do that.

Putting yellow irises on the table is another.

Monday after work I kicked the boys out on the sidewalk for a couple hours. Then I swept, mopped, vacuumed, even organized the laundry.

Forty-five minutes before going to the airport we all got in the shower.

The boys dressed up. I put on a white cotton sweater that my wife liked.

American Airlines, 7:50 p.m. Right on time. Herbie cried, "Mommy, Mommy" when she walked down the runway.

The girls were in fine form. The boys glad to see them. On our own, we're a good team, but together we win the championship.

Have luggage, will fly

I'm going to start a new group. An association for people who have had luggage fly off the top of their car.

We took the family up to the Bay area to visit friends who live in a little town east of Oakland called Lafayette. It's a town that, with the rest of the Bay area filling up, seems to be coming into its own.

The Bay area is beautiful. A breeze kept blowing in cool, salty air. The sun shone. And everything was either blue or green.

We hired a baby sitter for the kids and the four grown-ups went out to dinner in the city. We went to one of those grills that probably used to serve big juicy steaks but now feature spinach with goat cheese on it.

But I'm not complaining. It was a wonderful evening.

The wine flowed, the conversation raged, and people laughed as if they hadn't done so in years.

The weekend seemed to be building to a crescendo.

We decided to top the whole trip off by taking a trip to the San Francisco Zoo. The plan was for each family to take a separate car and after spending a couple hours at the zoo, we'd all eat, and then our group would drive back to Bakersfield.

Before leaving for the zoo, I tied four suitcases to the luggage rack on top of the car, just as I had done on the way up.

For tie-down purposes I used the Spider, which is eight bungee cords all tied together at the middle. Bungee cords are those stretchy cords with hooks on either end that kids use to tie their books to their bicycles.

The Spider had cost me $8.95 and had eliminated the need for the aggravating rope.

We caravaned to the zoo. Shortly after, hooking up with the 101 freeway off Route 80, I was jolted out of my driving trance by the scream of the 6-year-old in the back seat.

"Daddy, the suitcase fell off."

The suitcase fell off? Oh no! I looked in my rear-view mirror to see if I could pull over. Impossible. A semi was ready to eat my lunch.

I let the truck go by and then pulled over on the razor-thin shoulder. I got out and looked. Sure enough, we were short one suitcase. The blue canvas bag holding the kids' clothes had fallen off and was now being buffeted by three lanes of traffic.

It was a sobering sight.

Watching clothes being spread all over the road by Sunday-crazed motorists is like watching a shark tear into a school of tropical fish.

There wasn't much that could be done.

The fastest guy in the world couldn't

have retrieved that suitcase.

I walked back to the car, got in and said. "It's gone."

Silence.

"Do you realize that we're never going to see Herbie in his skeleton pajamas again?" my wife said. "And all of his Superman underwear was in there."

When we got to the zoo, our friends were, at first, silent. Who could blame them? What do you say to a guy who just had a suitcase blow off the top of his car? "Well, heck," said somebody searching for common ground. "I once had a suitcase stolen out of my car." "Did you ever have one blow off the top of your car?" I asked. "Well, I can't say that I have," Al answered.

The zoo was fine. Just great. I fit right in. I stopped in front of the monkey cage. I told the monkey if there was ever an opening, call me. He threw his head back and grinned, pointing to the rope hanging from the top of his cage.

T-ball

We recently finished our first experience with T-ball, the game that children today play before they get big enough for Little League.

Presumably this is a gentle way to learn baseball. Instead of being pitched, the ball rests sedately on a rubber tee. Teams do not keep score, which only heightens the curiosity about who won.

I knew my son's team, the Pirates, was in trouble when the coach called me at the beginning of the season.

"I want you to be my assistant coach," he said.

I patiently explained that I had never played baseball as a child, was not a softball enthusiast in my middle years and rarely watched the sport on TV.

"It doesn't matter," he said.

He wanted a body. A live one. Mine would do.

Native intelligence was not a qualification. When I had registered Herbie for the league, I left his birth certificate on the sign-up table. Now he won't be able to go to college or get married.

Before the season, we chose red shirts. We figured there was an intimidation factor in going with a strong primary color. The shirts arrived, but they were splashy canary yellow. It's a great color for a tuxedo or a large plane - and game shirts, our 15 Pirates decided.

I love the oversized baseball caps that make 7-year-olds look 5 again. The caps are the best thing about the team pictures. Ears stick out, and faces are plastered with winning grins.

The first practice was at a school near our house. I walked down with Herbie, eager to assume my assistant coaching duties. When we arrived, the boys were already playing catch and chasing ground balls. This was fun.

But wait a minute. There were two fathers out there with the coach shouting instructions, hitting ground balls and giving inspirational speeches on bended knee. It appeared that I had been relieved of my duties. Fired before the first practice.

I spent the rest of the season as an ardent supporter shouting such inanities as, "OK, guys, look sharp," as if a 7-year-old in the prime of his life would look dull.

My other favorite saying was "OK, get on your toes." A 7-year-old does not like to get on his toes, unless he's reaching for the cookie jar on the second shelf.

One of the truly outstanding things about T-ball was the snack bar. There were piping-hot churros, a pastry that's as long as a ruler and dusted with cinnamon sugar and thick with about 900 grams of fat. My favorite combination was a churro and a homemade tamale washed down by a Coke.

The baseball was entertaining. Innings ended with either three outs or one team scoring five runs. At the beginning of the season, outs were as rare as the Hope Diamond. If somebody caught a fly ball, he'd look at his mitt as if to ask, "How did you get in there?"

The highlight of Herbie's season came when he backhanded a screaming line drive at third base. He flashed a half-proud, half-scared smile at his mother and me sitting a few feet away.

His low point was getting clubbed in the neck by a kid on the other team who was practicing his home run swing. Forget this stuff about gentle.

T-ball was dangerous.

The best play of the season was when the intrepid shortstop on the Pirates stopped a hard ground ball with his face.

"Great play!" a woman screamed, almost coming out of her lawn chair. Turns out she had good reason to cheer because this was her son. She soon led him off the field with a handkerchief covering his bleeding nose.

The season's over and I'm ready to do it again. It was peaceful sitting out in the late afternoon sun watching children laugh, run around and chase home runs. You could be a good parent without ever having to leave your seat.

Homework

If you have kids, it's just a matter of time before you get involved with their homework. Up to now, my wife had done the duty. Last week it was my turn.

"Why don't you help Herbie make a hat out of newspaper?" Sue asked. "Get out 'Curious George Rides a Bike.' There is a diagram for a boat in there that could double as a hat."

"Good thinking," I replied, always relishing the opportunity to do something with my hands. "This will give Herbie and me a chance to work together."

My theory of homework is this: Unless you keep up with kids, they get ahead of you. Just the other day, Katie, as part of her homework, asked me to name five or more liquids. I wasn't even sure what they meant. Did they want something like liquid titanium or did cranberry juice count?

We opened up "Curious George," the wonderful story by H.A. Rey of the little monkey who means well but is irretrievably drawn to mischief. Halfway through the book, he helps a newsboy deliver papers, only to be charmed away from his responsibilities by two boys playing with their boats on a river.

He decided to make boats out of the newspaper. On pages 17 and 18 (just in case you want to give it a go), the author gives illustrated instructions on how to make the same four-cornered

boat/hat as George's.

"Herbie, go get some newspaper," I ordered, in firm control of this ship. "This will be a snap."

The instructions start like this. "First, take a newspaper. Fold it in half. Fold the corners down. Fold both edges up. Bring the ends together and flatten it sidewise."

We ground to a halt at the "flatten it sidewise." If I flattened our boat/hat sidewise, the newspaper didn't look like the one in the illustration. The book showed a square, but we had a triangle.

"Daddy, why are you stopping?" Herbie asked. "Is it finished yet?"

Nope, not finished. We were stuck on step four of 10 steps. Fifteen minutes had ticked by. I felt like the rat who keeps making the same wrong turn in the maze.

"Herbie, please get me some more newspaper," I asked quietly.

I started to get mad at Rey. I had a sneaking suspicion that the author had never made the boat himself and was merely exercising artistic license.

When a project gets sticky like this, it's important to show the child that you are firmly in control of both your emotions and the job. If the child loses confidence in you, he may opt for a substitute parent.

"Mommy, Daddy can't do this," Herbie said loudly.

"Herbie," I hissed. "Daddy is doing

just fine. There's just one tricky part."

I decided to ignore the drawing and go through the rest of the steps. We needed a finished product. The natives were getting restless.

"Daddy, that's not a hat," Herbie said.

"Are you going to wear that?" his sister asked, breaking out in a giggle.

By this time, the family had gathered around to see what the team had wrought. There was a hole for your head but the rest of it kind of slopped down around the ears. The end result wasn't that different from the guys at the races who, on sunny days, drape a newspaper over their heads.

"Get me a stapler," I said. You can fix anything with a stapler. We'd stiffen that baby up.

We did. Herbie pounded staples in. Pretty soon it was done.

He put it on. The hat covered his eyes, ears and nose. He was thrilled.

It wasn't much, but I'd put it up against anything the other parents came up with. From what I had heard, most kids weren't even doing their homework these days.

The next day we walked to school together. He wore the hat, carried his lunch box and sucked his thumb.

As we got closer to his classroom, I noticed a parade of children wearing brightly colored hats. There were ascots, derbies, bonnets and berets in all the colors of the rainbow. It was like that scene in the Fellini film where the peacock spreads its feathers in the snowstorm and all at once everything becomes very clear.

It was beautiful. Inspiring. Distressing.

I looked down at my 5-year-old wearing his newspaper hat. By now, the print was probably rubbing off on his forehead. What kind of father was I to put my kid in public with a hat like that?

He never even noticed. Not my cringing. Not the disparity between the models.

He had a hat. He and his daddy had made it. It covered his head.

I learned something in kindergarten that I hadn't learned the first time around. There is a family of hats just like there is a family of man. There are many colors, shapes and sizes. All are beautiful if the owner wears them with pride, grace and joy.

The first day of preschool

Our 2-year-old son started preschool. It's a good thing. Isn't it?

Put him up next to his 2-month old brother and, besides the obvious size difference, they're both babies. A big baby and a little baby. Each has real soft hands.

This preschool thing has been coming for awhile. Herbie has been doing more and more 2-year-old type things. Scaling furniture. Leaving a trail of toast around the house. Tearing apart rooms. And asking questions 'til your head is about to fall off.

Speeding the decision along has been a problem of playmates. No matter how many kids you have in a neighborhood, there never seems to be enough. Maybe that's because they're all in preschool. There you'll find 10 kids just like him. And the good thing is you don't have to clean up the mess.

At first, Herbie thought school was a great idea. You would, too, if your mother bought you a new red lunch box. And then your sister helped you decorate it with stickers.

The morning before school Herbie paraded around the house with his new lunch box. Big sister held his hand on the way out to the car and assured him that she would check in on him. He couldn't have cared less. He was going to school. We could jump in the nearest lake.

As we pulled up to the school, my son looked up to his mom and said, "I not cry." Then he took off for the door.

He looked into the classroom. The sea of strange faces caused a courage melt-down. Even the cookie hidden under his peanut butter and jelly sandwich would not save him now. "I don't want to go," Herbie wailed, thumb in mouth. "I want Mama." We said good-bye and left quickly.

A child is sometimes likened to a clean sheet of white paper. The first couple of years parents happily doodle around the edges. Gradually a picture appears. And although mothers and fathers want to be the primary artists, we soon enough discover that there are others who will push us aside.

We meet artists and would-be artists. All want a turn at the canvas. As the child grows up, there is less room for parents to add our little scribbles and notations. Soon we must fight our way through the crowd. Teachers, best friends, cartoon characters, neighbors and scout leaders all have their place at the drawing board.

I drove by the school at noon. I stopped, even though I told myself I shouldn't. The children were painting in the courtyard. Immersed in his painting, Herbie looked up only to show his handiwork to the teacher. It was a peaceful scene that required no parents.

It's no secret why I pulled over. You

grow to love the clean white paper with the delicately sketched edges. You get choosy about the artists. Worried about the outcome. You are sure no one is as good as you are.

The church bells rang, signaling me in some vague way to move on. I guess I had had my chance. And I shouldn't worry too much. With some help the painting will probably turn out fine.

The Tooth Fairy

I had scarcely hit the door after work when I found myself right in the middle of a family brouhaha. Katie, our 7-year-old, had swallowed her tooth.

Now, swallowing a tooth may not be as serious as, let's say, accidentally swallowing your keys, but that's not the point here. When you're 7, and you've been working on your tooth for a week, waiting for the right moment when it's going to pop loose on your pillow, then swallowing it is a heck of a lot more serious than swallowing some dumb keys.

There are things to worry about. The Tooth Fairy, for instance. How is she going to know that you lost your tooth unless she sees it underneath your pillow wrapped in a single tissue with a note taped to it? There are some things even the Tooth Fairy cannot take on faith and I think Katie realized that.

"Mommy, Mommy," she sobbed in her mother's arms, as close to inconsolable as she'd been in a while.

"What if the Tooth Fairy doesn't come?"

That is sad. That's kind of like Santa Claus not showing up.

A few minutes later we were given new reason to hope when Katie threw up all over her mother, the floor and the toilet. Not only was there a hearty representation of dinner, but who was to say the tooth had not come up to join the party?

"Mommy, do you think it's here?" she asked, her tears stilled for a moment.

"Your father will find out for you," said my wife firmly, in a voice comforting to everybody but me.

Boy, that's when you discover if you really love somebody. You want to find the tooth but you don't want to find the tooth.

I went to the rag bag, got two towels, came back and dropped to my knees. The more I looked and cleaned up, the more I realized just how much the Tooth Fairy will take on faith.

"Find anything yet?" my wife asked.

"No," I said. "But there's still the bathroom."

I remembered back to happier times. When Katie lost her first tooth the note read:

"Dear Tooth Fairy, please take special care of this tooth because it is very precious to me."

Taking this to heart, the Tooth Fairy wrote back, saying:

"Dear Katie, you have a beautiful tooth. I will put it in a very special place."

It wouldn't surprise me if she put that tooth in a little velvet box.

At the loss of her second tooth she wrote: "To the Tooth Fairy. I love you. When is your birthday? Tell me on a piece of paper. Love, Katie."

I finished cleaning the bathroom. No tooth.

Katie went to her desk to write another note. This one read:

"Dear Tooth Fairy, can you try to find my tooth? If you do, ansire (sic) my note. Love, Katie." At the bottom of the letter there were two empty boxes with "yes" or "no" written by them. The fairy was to check "yes" if she were able to and "no" if she were not.

The next morning Katie woke up and found a crisp new dollar under her pillow wrapped around a pretty new tooth. The Tooth Fairy has reserves. She had returned the note with a check in the "yes" box.

Bears

My friend Bart and I took our boys on a camping trip to Quaking Aspen, a mountain meadow that's a 90-minute drive from Porterville. The campground was full, save for two campsites. One was close to the road, noisy and dusty.

The other was beautiful.

It had a rock outcropping the kids could climb. Tall pine trees on a shaded slope fell away to a flowery meadow below. It had plenty of firewood. We couldn't figure out why it hadn't been taken.

We must have been lucky.

Shortly after unloading the gear, the kids discovered cute little chipmunks playing on the rocks. We made a trail of day-old microwave popcorn from the meadow up to the camp to entice the chipmunks to come closer. Later, I cut up an apple core into little pieces and scattered those, too.

The camp was happy. The kids played in the dirt, nightfall approached and a flock of brilliantly colored blue jays joined the chipmunks in eating the apple bits and popcorn.

After dinner, we took a walk in the meadow. One of the kids was acting up and we told him that if he didn't start behaving, we'd use him as bear bait. That quieted him down right away.

We went to bed early. When you have tents, going to bed early is a big deal.

I had one of those dreams induced by pork and beans and Raspberry Fig Newtons. In my dream, I was at work. A friend, who I hadn't seen in years, walked through the door. We embraced for what seemed like minutes in a bear hug. A bear hug.

A bear!

I woke up. There was a bear outside the tent. Four feet away. Lumbering around in the moonlight.

Holy Toledo.

You always imagine how you're going to be in those situations. Unselfish ("We must save the children first"). Or courageous ("Hand me my bear club, James"). Perhaps calm ("Panicking won't help things").

What I did was shiver and contemplate tossing one of the kids out of the tent. All I could think of was: Please don't carry me away, Mr. Bear.

You've heard the expression "little brown bear." Well, forget it. Bears are not little. Even little bears are bigger than you want them to be.

How big was that bear? Well, the first thing I thought was gorilla. No, after turning his massive head in my direction, I decided to upgrade my assessment to mastodon.

What should I do? Announce

myself and inform Mr. Bear that we had no food. Yes, that was the courteous thing to do.

But wait a minute. What if he didn't know we were there? Telling him we were there would be like adding one more special to the menu.

I decided to keep quiet. I didn't want to wake up the kids but, more importantly, I didn't want to have a confrontation the bear was sure to win.

I looked around the tent to see what kind of weapons were available. Besides a flashlight, the most potent weapon I had was a little toy chainsaw made by Mattel with a pull string that made the blade vibrate. My only hope was to brandish it and hope the bear laughed himself to death.

Fortunately, the bear lumbered uphill to where Bart and his little boy were sleeping. I hoped that if the bear did eat Bart, he would at least leave the keys to the Bronco. I liked Bart, but when Mr. Bear comes, friendship becomes secondary.

The bear stopped at the Little Igloo ice chest on the picnic table, the only food container we had out. He started pounding it against what sounded like a tree. He couldn't open it. Mr. Bear was angry. He knew there was food in the camp, he just didn't know where.

Five minutes later, he left.

Two hours later, another bear came through. These bears clearly were not communicating. This was just the apple and popcorn stop. The honey was in the next camp.

Meanwhile, the kids slept and Bart and I wondered when morning was going to come. The only problem with going to bed early is that morning doesn't come soon enough.

We found out why that camp didn't have any people. It had been voted Camp Most Likely To Be Visited By Bears.

Checking with other campers the next day revealed that we were the only camp blessed with the big beasts. I guess we had the bare necessities.

The Miracle of Sod

Like many American men, I spend most of my waking hours in mortal fear that my grass is going to die.

My wife thinks I am a nut. With all the things to worry about in the world - perpetual famine in Africa, rain forests without wood and our own precarious financial situation - why do I spend hours trolling my lawn, cursing the explosive weed growth of the last few weeks, despairing when I see a bald spot?

I think a man feels the same way about his lawn as he does his hairline. No one likes losing his hair, and any man who tells you that baldness is a sign of virility is either lying, bald or both. A bald man may be virile, but what he is more than anything else is bald.

I thought my problems were over this spring when I put in sod. People who have laid sod get this beatific look on their face when they describe its pleasure, and now I understand why. It's like getting a really good hairpiece. People say, "I know he's got a wig on, but it's expensive."

Our back yard had been a disgrace. We had some grass, but mostly the yard was dirt. Brown, ugly dirt. In a place like Bakersfield, you don't need any more brown, ugly dirt.

I called the sod man. I found myself gushing out all my lawn problems to this stranger. He was trying to sell a little sod and get off the phone and I wouldn't let him.

"Make sure you get the lawn level," he said. "Otherwise you'll regret it in a couple of years."

It didn't take a couple of years to start regretting my interest in a lawn that isn't level. It started that night at dinner when I went public with my feelings about a lawn with slope.

"I've never really cared for a level lawn," I said. "I think they look too sterile. I like contours."

Silence. "I'd prefer it level," Sue said.

The conversation was over. The work wasn't.

Anybody who has messed with lawns knows that to get level ground you have to run something called a rototiller over it. This chews up the soil, which you then remove by the trainload from your would-be lawn. The rototiller, which doesn't weigh any more than 600 pounds, works better if you walk backward on your tiptoes like a ballerina. It's like trying to waltz with the bear at the circus when he is trying to get back in his cage.

I wouldn't say rototilling my lawn was as hard as heaving hay bales onto a flatbed truck, but it's a heck of a lot harder than any of the sissy work I've done lately.

I'll tell you what, though, once the dirt was wet and the sod was down, I felt like a new man.

It's gorgeous. There isn't one weed to be seen. It's thick and green.

It looks wonderful, it looks fantastic and it looks too good to last.

The last couple of days I've noticed the sod dying out around the swing set. The kids have already worn grooved places dragging their feet under the swings, but we expected that.

On a more chilling note, I have noticed patches of grass completely apart from the swing set not doing well. I hope that's just the rye grass dying out and the Bermuda coming in.

It makes me wonder if a lawn has a soul, a preconceived set of instructions, and no matter what you do to it, it always returns to its original state.

A friend down the street came over and said, "Sod, that's a great idea. We've done it three times in the last 10 years."

Meanwhile, I've got problems with some of the 96 sprinklers that keep the lawn alive. Some aren't working, and I don't know which ones they are because they run in the middle of the night and I've never really figured out my automatic sprinkler system.

Every morning I wake up to dry spots and I feel like the detective who shows up for the murder after they've taken the body away. I am always tempted to go back to the old spray-the-lawn-with-a-hose system. But that's lame, it's like admitting that you'll never get the hang of your sprinkler system.

This summer is going to get ugly, I know, and I dread the war ahead of me. Grass is just waiting to die. I must keep it alive at all costs.

The jog-a-thon

As proud parents of a Franklin School first-grader, we are supporters of just about everything the school has to offer.

Candy bar sale? We'll take a dozen. Yum Yum Day? Yes, my wife will be there to make change and pass out Cornuts, licorice and Fun Fruits. Door knobbies? Sure, give me a few of those furry devils.

The jog-a-thon was no different. I'm sure you're familiar with the concept. A child gets family members and friends to pledge so much money per lap.

It works like this. Say you pledge 50 cents a lap and this child runs three laps. You owe $1.50. The Franklin jog-a-thon goal was to raise money for new playground equipment. When Katie brought home the sign-up sheet and asked us to make our pledge, we asked her how many laps she thought she could do.

I think she said five. Not wanting to appear cheap, her mother signed up at $1.50 a lap. I pledged $1.

That night we called her grandparents in Arizona. Great idea, they said with a laugh. Put us down for $4 a lap.

We called my parents. They went for a flat $10. Nothing per lap.

A couple of days later, Katie and I walked over to Franklin School after work. There were six or seven kids milling around so I organized a relay race. This gave me a chance to watch Katie run around the 300-yard track.

What a pretty runner. Definitely a half-miler, though. She looked great for 150 yards and then did the final 150 on guts.

The evening of the jog-a-thon, my wife met me at the door with a worried look on her face. I asked her how the day had gone.

"Fine, except Katie ran 17 laps," she replied.

Seventeen laps. No. Normally if your little first-grader runs 17 laps, you're happy. But as far as I was concerned, Katie was on probation.

"We're in it for $42.50," my grieving wife said. "But worse than that, my parents owe $68. My dad's going to flip."

"Wait a second," I said calmly. "They don't have to send $68. Just have them send $20 or something. We'll just call Franklin and tell them we had no idea."

"We can't," she replied. "Franklin's not the company who handles the bill."

I could see this one coming. Grandpa doesn't pay his bill and they throw him in collections. Grandpa is a retired credit manager with Sears. If he fears anything worse than death, it's a bad credit rating.

No, Grandpa had to pay his bill. Or Grandpa was going to jail.

At dinner that night, I asked Katie how she was able to run 17 laps. "Oh, Daddy. Once I got the hang of it, I didn't care. I felt good out there," she answered enthusiastically.

You sure looked like it.

"And, Daddy, some nice men were cheering us on. They were giving us ice and cherry drinks," she said, barely able to contain herself.

Those men wouldn't happen to work for ABC school promotions, would they?

As part of the day's festivities Katie bought a T-shirt ($5) that read, "I survived the Franklin School Jog-a-thon." We should buy one for Katie's grandpa in Arizona. He might think it's funny. Then again, he might not.

New clothes

I bought new clothes in January. No smart person wants to die, so I figured if I brought home some clothes I'd have a decent chance of living forever.

How does this make sense? Well, there is something about dressing up that makes one feel immortal. Like he or she can do no wrong.

But it's more than that. This is a spiritual issue. As the musical group Earth, Wind and Fire said in a song, there is your inner self and your outer self. My outer self needed some work.

High water pants? I got 'em. And plenty of nice shirts with holes in the armpits.

I am the hand-me-down king. I have a whole closet of clothes that almost fit. The kind of clothes that people make remarks about, as in: "That's a nice coat. It almost fits you."

For example, two years ago I got this great deal on a camel-hair coat from a tailor who had ended up with it when a customer skipped town. This is one step above buying clothes from a dead man. This jacket almost worked. I looked like a guy who had lost weight but his clothes hadn't.

I'd fit right in, if I lived in a town called Dorkville.

No more. After Christmas, I hit the sales. Did the catalogs. I wanted to get right.

Do you know what happens when I buy new clothes? I get fussy. I care more than you should about the strengths and weaknesses of light starches, drip drying and low heat.

I obsess.

Last week, I spent five minutes trying to decide between my blue Viyella socks or the old standard grays. Right now, I'm mad at one of my sweaters because it rubbed black cottonballs on one of my new white shirts.

I know I'm spending valuable spiritual energy on clothes, but I can't help it. I am shallow now and prefer it that way.

The other day I was wearing this turquoise green turtleneck that I got from L.L. Bean. It's gorgeous. Everybody loves it. Anyway, I'm carrying our 10-month-old baby out the back door and I accidentally brush against the door.

Rrriiippp. Some person had left a small nail in the door. A Christmas wreath went on that nail during the holidays, but the wreath was gone and the nail wasn't.

I looked down at my left sleeve where a quarter-inch of material used to be. I might as well rip the whole shirt into strips for polishing silver.

Before dinner that evening, I was working in the garage working on a bike derailleur with cleaning fluid. I had forgotten to take off my new brown leather shoes. I must have splashed gas on them, because when I sat down for dinner, I noticed an ugly black splotch on the left shoe.

Maybe spit would work? Nope. How about a dry napkin? How about a bow and arrow?

I could barely lift my eyes to the plate. Would someone tell me why the dinner conversation was so lively? What was everybody so happy about? How could people be talking to me when my new shoe had become an old shoe?

The next morning I got up, picked up the shoes and noticed there was a small X etched into the top of my right shoe. What! Where did that come from?

It was the kind of X a small boy would carve to indicate that hidden treasure was nearby. I have three boys and all of them, including the baby, were now suspects.

I don't get it. Are new clothes haunted? Is there some little devil sitting there guiding you into every nail, through every patch of oil, straight in the path of every runaway mustard truck?

Or is this life's way of getting even. Leveling the playing field. Reminding us not to place the wrong emphasis on the wrong thing.

Before I turn myself back over to religion, I just want to know one thing: How does Richard Gere do it? His white suit is always white.

I just want to be right for one day. I want to be smooth, well-dressed, well-spoken, funny, a conscientious father, a great friend, an Italian stallion. The way my inner self has been behaving lately, it may be my only shot at immortality.

Composting

I bought a composter that looks like nothing but an extra wide trash can without a bottom. It has air vents on the sides. A sliding door at ground level.

Now you may wonder at a time when Nicaragua is in the throes of democratic turmoil, Eastern Europe is getting ready to slug it out in the free marketplace and Libya is producing chemical weapons, why anybody would want to think about composting?

Because the world is moving too fast. In the case of Lithuania declaring its independence, that's good. But for you and me sprinting headlong through our lives, that may not be so good.

Composting is slow. It takes six to eight weeks to break down whatever combination of leaves, wood ashes, and table scraps you put into it. There's no hurrying the process.

Most people compost because they want to improve their soil. Enrich their gardens. Grow prize-winning tomatoes.

I wanted to do something about the mountain of bread crusts that our family creates. The kids eat their peanut butter and jelly sandwiches without the crusts on. The crusts perish in the white garbage bags or get ground up in the disposal. It seemed a waste.

One day a neighbor gave me an impromptu tour of her two composters. "We put all our kitchen scraps in here," she told me excitedly. She showed me the eggshells, coffee grounds, grapefruit halves, banana peels and bread crusts. Then we walked through her garden which contains some of the richest, darkest soil around.

Boom. I ordered one. Ninety-nine dollars.

"You paid $99 for a trash can?" said a couple of friends. "You could make one of these for $10. You could also dig a hole in the back yard and cover it with chicken wire and compost that way."

I took some grief, but my marriage can't stand a hole in the back yard covered with chicken wire. And if I have to pay an extra 40 bucks for a container blessed by the compost masters, fine.

The first thing I did was put out a dictum to the crustwasters.

"Save those crusts," I said like a man in charge. "They're going in the composter. We'll use everything but meat scraps and greasy things."

Then I cleaned out the ashes from the fireplace. Gathered up the leaves from the flower beds. A neighbor donated his grass clippings. I added some secret magic starter mix and we were ready to cook up a batch.

A week later, I went out to put the previous night's dinner scraps in the compost bin. As per the instructions, I drove the composting tool to the bottom and mixed the bottom mush with the newly added asparagus stalks and wilted marigolds.

The stuff from the bottom was steaming. I put my hands into the dark mixture. It was warm. Almost alive.

I called the kids over and they stuck their hands in it. Talk about thrilling. We were part of "the great chain of life" or something like that.

Weeks still fly by. But now, it's not the melancholy feeling of "where does the time go?" It's "we're one week closer to victory." Time is an ally. You may be getting older, but so is your compost.

My friend Pete might liken it to the pleasures of a savings account. It works while you sleep, watch TV and ride your bike.

Well, I got so revved up about the whole thing, that I've told 10 people. A neighbor got one and when I saw her last week she was really excited.

"It's steaming," she said. "It's already steaming."

This is not a solution to the Sandinista situation. It won't ease Poland's transition to capitalism. And it won't do anything about the Middle Eastern leader with his finger on the trigger.

But for those sandwich crusts that drive you crazy, it's just the thing.

There is pleasure in it. Watching things break down. Watching things grow.

Plumbing

The Thanksgiving holiday started out on a challenging note when the kitchen sink drain clogged up Wednesday night.

"Mom put spinach stems down the disposal," my wife whispered timidly when I came home from work. "I'm sorry."

No need to be sorry because I'm not going to rake my mother-in-law over the coals. This woman is the Magic Johnson of mothers-in-law. She has bad games, but not very often.

Plus, I like working on the plumbing. I've been under the sink before and I can assure you that there is nothing to fear.

"I'll fix it," I said quietly.

Quietly, that's a good place to start when you begin a plumbing job. The thing you don't want to do is to become anxious, lose your cool and break a pipe with brute strength.

A few months ago, potato skins clogged up the drainage disposal and it took me 10 minutes to clean out the skins and three hours to reconnect the disposal. I came close to snapping off pipe that disappears into the wall.

This time I had my father-in-law around to help. I figured that no one could live as long as he has and know less than I do. Anyway, the project would give us something to do together.

Take out the old screwdrivers. Get grease on our hands. Talk to one another in deep voices.

Just the kind of thing men like to do together.

I quickly unscrewed the pipe that connected the drainage disposal to the outside lines and brought it up so that Dad could look at it.

"Any obstruction in there, John?" I asked lightly.

"No," he responded.

Well, well, well, I thought. I guess this means that the pipe in the wall is clogged up. You know the pipe that's buried in 40 feet of concrete. The one you have to jackhammer to get to it.

I walked down two houses where Jack, the plumbing contractor, lived. Jack came to the door dressed casually, smelling of aftershave. I asked him if he could help. The question should have been, "How would you like to come out of your warm house at 10 o'clock on Thanksgiving eve and unclog my sink for the next 1-1/2 hours?"

If he helped me, maybe I could do the same for him. I found it difficult to imagine what I could possibly help Jack with. "Hey, Jack, you need a little help with your essay?" I guess I could offer to wash his truck sometime.

Jack went into his garage to get the plumber's snake, which is a coil-like thing that works its way through blocked pipes. They come in all sizes and evidently this one wasn't big enough because, after 30 minutes of trying, Jack gave up and said, "Can you wait till tomorrow? I'll go to the shop and get the big snake."

That night we washed the dishes in the bathtub, which is actually a pretty good place to wash dishes. There's plenty of room and the water pressure's great. It also has a pioneer-on-the-prairie kind of feel.

Thanksgiving morning I was out getting the paper when I saw Ron, another neighbor, who is a building contractor. Jack didn't appear to be up yet, so I thought maybe I'd save him a trip to the shop. I described the problem to Ron and asked him what he would do.

"Get a garden hose, put it into the pipe, seal it with towels and then turn it on full blast. You may knock the crud loose. It works every time for me."

That sounded like a great idea to me and my father-in-law, the dynamic duo, so we brought a hose through the window, stuffed it in the pipe in the wall and sealed it with towels.

"Turn it on," I yelled.

I thought we had her for a moment but all of a sudden a small tidal wave surged out of the hole, over my shoes and onto the floor. I looked up and noticed water cascading out of the air vent pipe on top of the house. You tell me how that happened.

"Turn it off," I screamed.

Jack came over later that morning with the big snake. Two hours later, we had cut through the crud in the pipe. Excuse me, did I use the word we? That's kind of like a Laker fan saying that we beat Boston.

Jack beat Boston. I was just trying to act helpful.

It was a surprisingly good way to spend Thanksgiving. No one got mad. Dad and I got to get out the tools together and chum around a little bit.

And Thanksgiving dinner tasted good. That plumbing work, it really gives you an appetite.

The moving blues

When I picked up our second-grader from school, she burst into tears.

"Daddy, I'm never going to see Christie again," Katie sobbed, tears rolling down her freckled cheeks. "Tonight she's moving to Texas."

The "tonight" is something that really kills me about kids. Their experience with the world is so immediate that tonight and the rest of their lives are synonymous.

But no one was paying me to sit in the driver's seat to philosophize in silence. This was one of those pivotal times for a parent when one is expected to pull out some comforting bit of wisdom.

"Why is Christie moving to Texas?" I asked, searching for solid ground.

"Because her dad got transferred there," she said, laying the blame on Christie's dad.

"It's OK to cry," I said, echoing a poor line in a bad movie.

Katie cried harder. She was beyond sappy movies and half-truths.

"Just think, you'll have another person to visit in Houston," I said, making reference to her best friend who had moved two years before. Katie had so many friends in Texas that she might as well move there.

"And you'll have somebody else to write to," I added, at once suspecting that Katie wasn't in the market for a new correspondent.

What was it about Houston? Everyone was moving there. A guy at work; two of Katie's friends, and Paulette, the balloon lady. California used to be like that, a place people moved to.

Moving. It's hard to explain to kids because most of us are still trying to put it together ourselves. Moving - like death - is one of those things people around you do that you wish they wouldn't. They never give you enough notice and they leave you alone to deal with the quiet.

There is no purer sorrow than losing a friend to a move. When you are a child, it is the loss of that daily contact. The lunches shared in the shade of a mulberry tree. The swinging side by side in the winter sky.

Secrets shared before being picked up from school. Brownie projects. A funny thing that your little brother said that only she can appreciate because she has one just like him.

It doesn't matter if your friend is moving across town or across the world. It hurts. And all the philosophy and the correspondence and the planned trips don't make it hurt any less.

When you first find out, you want to blame somebody, lay yourself in front of the moving van, put the words back in their mouths. In the words of a boy who lost his mother: "You wish it was yesterday."

I wish I could have told Katie that it gets easier as she gets older, but I couldn't. What happens is that you get used to the sensation of being hollowed out. It's like beating a piece of meat until it gets tender. People leave so often, you begin to think that it's not the accident you first imagined.

Mature people develop game faces and stock answers. "Oh, Jim's leaving. Sounds like a real step up careerwise.

I understand there's nothing like the wildflowers on the Wyoming plains."

A few minutes later, Katie stopped crying. It had nothing to do with what I said or didn't say. Tears, like friendships, run their course. Hers was a child's way of going forward.

A must, even for the big kids.

Anyway, there were letters to compose. A new name to put in the address book. And memories to file in the most precious of places.

Making bread

Dee came over to my desk and said, "How's the column going?" What column do you mean, dear? I silently snarled at the delightful woman who lays out my column and does 10 million other things as well.

Do you mean the column that was due three days ago? Do you mean the one I haven't started yet? Is that the one you mean?

December brings its own brand of testiness. Days are shorter, schedules are tighter and blown fuses are only an askance look away.

Dee wants my column. My response to that is to sulk, get up from the desk, go home and make bread.

Yes, make bread.

In the winter, when I feel the heaviness laying on my heart and the steely fingers tightening around my neck, my response is to check the fridge for some yeast, the flour canisters for whole wheat and the pantry for honey.

I suspect my male friends might be thinking, "He makes bread? Is this the feminine side of his personality coming out? He'll be getting colored underwear next."

Let me say one thing to you, oh snake-stomping, can-chewing, mustache-wearing friends of mine. Women love a man who makes bread.

Have you ever seen how many women hang out around bakeries? A ton of them. And it's not just the lemon custard doughnuts.

But I'm not trying to pick up women when I make bread. I'm escaping the world and there is no better way than to make bread. Whole wheat bread.

I've experimented. There's Monday Pumpernickel, but how about if it's Tuesday? Milk and honey bread is finished too quickly. It's not bread unless it takes about nine hours of your day. That means it's got to rise twice.

The first thing to do is boil milk and let it cool to room temperature. Do you know how pleasant it is to have milk steaming away in your kitchen? Time stretches out because milk takes its time to cool.

Do you want to please your family? After you mix the yeast (a magical substance if there ever was one), cooled milk and melted butter, put in double the called-for amount of honey. No one likes dry, plain bread. Think cake.

Then it's time to throw in five cups of whole wheat flour. But here's the place to cheat again. Yes, put in a couple cups of whole wheat flour so your bread will have that brown color associated with healthful bread, but substitute some white flour and oatmeal for the brown stuff. This helps your bread avoid that Desert Storm consistency.

After mixing comes one of those highlights of the bread-making experience: kneading. This can be as satisfying as giving a good massage. The bread is now satiny smooth and pulls together like a good NFL secondary. It is ready to be put in a warm place to rise.

I'm going to tell you a little secret. Sure, you can put the dough in a warm oven and it will swell to twice its size in a hurry, but that is not nearly spiritual enough.

What you want to do is light a fire in the fireplace and place the bowl covered with a fresh towel beside it. There's something about that radiant heat. Fire, bread - all you need is a hymn book and a knitting project and you're about there.

The last time I put the bread dough by the fireside, a molten log launched a fiery ember on top of the cloth and burned a hole right through it.

After the bread rises to twice its size, roll it and divide it into two parts, each to go in its own bread pan. Don't wrench the dough apart with the force you would trying to remove the head of a chicken. Twist gently, as if trying to pick a stubborn pomegranate.

Bread baking in the oven is one of the best smells in the world. It has to be on the list with spring flowers and teriyaki jerky.

No one can wait for the bread to cool before cutting thick slabs. On cool bread, butter won't melt and spread. Yes, butter. Skip the margarine. Use that on the store-bought stuff.

It's the best bread you'll ever eat. Almost the best food.

Last week I made some bread and walked half a loaf of it across the street to some neighbors.

"Slice it real thin in the morning and toast it up for your kids," I instructed. "They'll love it."

I came over the next morning after breakfast. Two pieces of thinly sliced whole wheat bread sat on plastic plates.

"The kids didn't eat a bite," my neighbor said sheepishly. "They prefer white bread."

HERB'S WHOLE WHEAT BREAD
1-2/3 cups milk
3 cups whole wheat flour
1 cup oatmeal
1-1/2 cups white flour
2 tablespoons butter, melted
3 shakes of salt
1 bright yellow yeast package
1 cup honey
Handful of wheat germ (very optional)

Heat the heck out of the milk and then let cool to room temperature. Put yeast into 1/4 cup of warm water (if it's too hot for a bath, then it's too hot for the yeast and will kill it). Add yeast-water mixture to milk and then keep right on adding the honey, salt, melted butter and about four cups of the flour.

Beat like you're mad at it. Then add the rest of the flour, oatmeal and anything else I haven't already mentioned. Sprinkle flour on the chopping block (not the one you cut onions on) and turn dough onto the block, kneading it like there's no tomorrow. After five minutes, quit, put dough in greased bowl and put bowl in warm place.

Let rise for 1-1/2 hours or until it's grown big enough to scare young children. Then turn it back on the wood block, puncture, elongate and divide into two handsome loaves. Place two handsome loaves into two handsome bread pans, greased of course, and put back into warm place and let rise for another 45 minutes.

Bake in a preheated oven at 375° for about 45 minutes or until top of bread is brown.

Recycling

Are you as tired of recycling as I am?

I'm to the point where I want to contribute to the landfill problem. Burn leaves in the street. Live a generally carefree and irresponsible existence.

It's not that I'm against recycling, because I'm not. We recycle, sometimes even cheerfully.

We have six blue Rubbermaid trash bins in our back yard. Each is neatly stenciled: newspaper, cardboard, green glass, clear glass, plastics and aluminum cans.

When I started recycling, I was a rational human being. Then I caught the recycling virus. Now I find myself rescuing Kleenex boxes out of the bathroom trash bin. My wife faithfully washes out peanut butter jars - less fun than cleaning the dog dish.

The problem becomes: Where do you draw the line? Cardboard boxes are one thing, but how about the "rolling thing inside the toilet paper," as a friend of mine calls it?

He, of course, is referring to the cardboard toilet paper tube. I like to think of it as a trumpet in those spontaneous musical moments, but when you catch the recycling virus, you recycle the toilet paper tube. Otherwise the recycling police will come and arrest you.

Recycle, and things stack up like you can't believe.

Every two weeks I hoist the trash cans up into my truck and drive to the recycling center behind Pepper Tree Market. The container with the cardboard is almost weightless and the trash can with clear glass weighs about 3,000 tons.

Sometimes, I'll grab the cardboard one thinking it's the glass one and nearly throw it over the Montgomery Ward building.

I am assisted at the recycling center by my 5-year-old son, Sam. His favorite part is trying to break the cranberry juice bottles as he drives them home into the center of the bin.

After recycling, we drive home with six trash cans - now considerably lighter - rolling around in the back of the truck. Every so often one of the lids will fly off and cause an innocent motorist to run into a large pole.

Not only do we recycle, but we compost. This earthy practice involves scraping the scrambled eggs, raisin toast, oatmeal and broccoli remains into a piece of handsome Tupperware near the kitchen sink.

When large birds begin roosting in the kitchen window, it's time to transport the scraps out to the composter, a brown, squat plastic container that looks a little like a robot without a head.

Does the food break down and become rich, crumbly soil? No. It just lies there and looks sad.

What I really do in my $99, made-in-Canada compost bin, is raise insects. These include giant winged ones, two varieties of flies - fruit and house - and, of course, ants. Between meals, the ants will sometimes travel the three feet into our bathroom window and host a parade around the bathtub.

So I am a recycler and I can complain about being a recycler.

I mentioned my feelings about recycling to a friend and he agreed:

"Aren't we done with that one yet?" he asked. "I'm waiting till we get to the point where we've recycled everything and I can start throwing things away again."

In the meantime, I recommend cheating occasionally. Yesterday, I threw away a Honey Nut Cheerios box. I could feel the pleasure coursing through my hands like a good golf swing.

Next on my list is the peanut butter jar.

Patriotism

Judy Warren, a Red Lion Inn employee, quit after a dispute with her boss.

No big deal. It happens every day. Somebody tangles with a supervisor and has his or her momentary flirtation with human dignity and pulls the old take-this-job-and-shove-it routine.

This one was different and got a lot of attention because Warren wanted to display an American flag at her desk. Her boss, a native of Jordan named Imad Abu-Alya, told her to take it down.

She quit because not only did she feel she was mistreated but, as Warren said, "I can't work for a man who is against the things I believe in, and the flag is one of those things."

The town was whipped into a frenzy by the media. Folks were outraged at this apparent absence of patriotism at a time when patriotism is held in especially high esteem. Assemblyman Trice Harvey said, "I wouldn't want to work for that jerk, either."

Public opinion didn't soften when Warren claimed Abu-Alya was a supporter of Saddam Hussein.

People picketed the Red Lion. The hotel, catching an instant whiff of some major-league public relations problems, dusted off all the flags it had in inventory and offered Warren her job back. On Monday, the hotel decided not to rehire Warren and reassigned Abu-Alya to another post.

I had an uneasy feeling the first time I heard the story. It seemed too cut and dried. My sense, and I was not alone among some co-workers or readers, was that there might be another side that didn't make Abu-Alya look like a Jordanian strongman.

In my opinion, the story seemed unbalanced. There was a hysterical tone to some of the quotes. The public reaction had all the trimmings of a lynching party with some poor guy saying, "But wait a minute, I didn't do it," as they threw the rope over his neck.

There has never been a real good time in this country to be something other than a WASP, but now may be the worst. Especially if you have a hyphenated last name and you look toward the East for your morning blessings.

Maybe this guy made a mistake. He denied this woman a chance to put up the flag at a time when flying flags provide comfort for millions of citizens and inspiration for thousands of soldiers. You can't take that away from people, not in this country.

But even if Abu-Alya made a mistake, does he deserve to get run out of town? He was reassigned. That sounds better, but he had to leave because it was starting to feel like Mississippi in the '20s. Or New York

City in the late '80s.

No one here has had any luck getting the other side of the story because Red Lion employees are scared to death to talk. The hotel wants to get back to business, and being in the news doesn't help.

The newspaper received calls from people who claimed they worked for the Red Lion. They wanted to talk but were not willing to do so on record. Anonymous sources and closed lips are death to newspaper articles.

So, in the dark, it withers away. We are left with Warren's version of the story, which may or may not be complete.

I remain uneasy. What is the implication here: That if somebody doesn't fly a flag, put ribbons around their trees, or fully agree with the way the American government is handling this or any other matter, a man or woman should fear for his or her life?

Probably not. This is a better-than-decent system. It encourages discussion and welcomes dissent. America is a pretty wonderful place to be.

Unless your skin is dark. And you have a hyphenated last name. And you are anxiously awaiting news of family and loved ones.

Then it might be wise to keep your head down. Stay quiet. Mind your own business and avoid political discussions.

You don't believe it? Ask Abu-Alya, wherever he may be.

Juliet Thorner

I had coffee with Juliet Thorner and it was the tonic I needed. There's nothing better than an old doctor who is full of wisdom.

Dr. Juliet Thorner was one of the first female pediatricians in Bakersfield. She began her practice in 1937 when there were all of 35 doctors in town.

My memories of Dr. Thorner center around her sunny Westchester office. She took care of me, my two sisters and three brothers, and thousands of other children over the years. She took care of us until we were 12 or so, at which time she would give her famous "You're getting too old to come see me anymore" speech.

Even though I knew it was coming, that speech still broke my heart. I'd grown to like this energetic woman whose voice could be heard in an examining room three doors down the hall. She made going to the doctor easy.

During my teen-age years, I lost track of her. But as I grew older, I heard bits and pieces of news about her. I knew she'd retired from practice in 1975 and had gone to work for the Kern County Health Department.

But about a year ago, she had gotten sick. Cancer. She had an operation, and now is recovering from the surgery.

That's where I picked up on her life again, one cold, overcast Bakersfield day. Hunched over and smaller than I

remember, we hugged and she thanked me for visiting. But it was I who should have been thanking her for the gift she gave me that day.

There was a fire in the fireplace. A bowl of mixed nuts sat on the glass table, along with two china cups and a pot of fresh coffee.

How someone can take the menace out of pancreatic cancer and the ensuing operation I do not know. But she did. Not by minimizing the danger (this type of cancer is usually fatal and the surgery is difficult), but by maximizing its potential.

"It is a very long operation," Thorner said. "At the beginning of the surgery, I got a very strong feeling that I was going to be granted more time to live to do the work I had to do. From that moment, the rest of the experience was thrilling.

"After the operation an old nemesis of mine, a man I really had problems with professionally, came through the door. We visited for two hours. I found out he had had cancer some years before."

Juliet Thorner has reached the state of mind where everything is a blessing, no matter how deep the cut or problematic the recovery. This had not always been the case. But in 1975, after a serious bout with hepatitis, Thorner converted to Christianity.

For a woman of science who had

spent her life in study and practice, this was quite a conversion. She has spent the past 11 years exploring her faith and sorting out what she believes in from what she does not.

Thorner has been an active parishioner. A member of the First Baptist Church, she has set up a program to reach out to people who live alone. This means calling and checking on them once a day. According to Thorner, most of the time the folks just need to hear a friendly voice.

As the fire burned down, I realized that this woman, fresh from surgery, had already recovered in a practical sense. She had what she needed - more time. The less-than-two-years the doctor gave her was enough to do what she had to do.

Shed no tears for Juliet Thorner. She's found what she's been looking for. It took her 75 years. And now she has the rest of her life to enjoy it.

New sprinklers, old sprinklers

There is a learning curve when you move into a 50-year-old house. You develop a strategy and a long list to deal with the house's idiosyncracies. Item one for me was the grass strip in front of our house.

The strip didn't have sprinklers. I had spent last summer watching the lawn turn brown and die. I resolved to put in sprinklers when the weather turned cooler. With water, that brown strip would stay lovely and green year-round.

When discussing irrigation, especially home irrigation, the word often raised is coverage. This concept can be compared to the Hands Across America fund-raiser several years ago. To have a strong chain, your sprinklers must touch one another. If there is a gap, a hole, you can expect an ant pile.

Two weeks ago, our gardener and I met to develop a plan. He was charged with buying the plastic pipe, fittings and sprinkler heads. I, on the other hand, would supply the brute labor necessary to dig the trenches.

Last Saturday, I took a shovel and lightly walked toward the front lawn. The birds were singing. It was a beautiful day for physical labor.

Tell me, is there anything more honest than digging a ditch? The sweat glistens on the brow, there is clean brown dirt on one's pant leg and little children keep a respectful distance.

Can you call it work? Within an hour, I had dug a handsome ditch, a foot square, with a dogleg left around one tree and a dogleg right around another one.

It was pretty.

Two days later, the gardener came over to put in the system. While I was at work, he put it in without hooking it up. When I got home, we marveled at the clean white pipe and the seven new sprinkler heads.

Coverage, we laughed. We had coverage.

Since the sun was going down, I told him to wait till tomorrow to button it up. We gave each other the thumbs-up sign as he drove away.

The next morning at work I got a call from my wife. She was excited. Something had gone wrong with the project.

"Did you know that there was already a line in that strip?" she asked.

"Did it ever occur to you to check it before going and spending $100?" she asked, slowly picking up steam.

"No, you have to go off half-cocked ..."

The phone was warm in my hand. I tried to say something dignified. But to say something dignified, you must be thinking something dignified. All I could think was, "Oh, no."

I told her I'd be home in a couple of minutes.

When I pulled up, the gardener was shaking his head.

"I can't believe it," he said. "There's a whole other line buried in the lawn. I've been cutting this grass for almost a year. I can't believe I haven't seen it."

He noticed my wife standing on the porch with a dark expression. "I can't blame you," he said, loud enough for her to hear. "I'm the gardener."

That was nice of him not to blame me. Of course, he was in no danger of getting fired. I was in no danger of getting fired. I was already fired.

We decided to investigate the system, this being as good a time as any.

We soon found two more turn-on valves. Not only did the strip have sprinklers, but it turned out that the front lawn had the most thorough system for which one could hope.

I had had enough sprinkler heads and lines to water all of Jastro Park.

And now I had double that amount.

Well, let's look at the positive side. Like a twin-engine airplane, I now have two systems. If one breaks down, I can go to the other one. In case an earthquake hits one of the lines, I'll still have coverage.

That makes me feel good.

Or you can look at it another way. I'll be a very popular guy with my friends the next time we need earthworms for a fishing trip. Heck, with such a well-watered lawn, I'll have enough worms for the whole river.

So, as you can see, I had my reasons. It just took a little digging.

If you ever have a problem with coverage or if you want to put in a dual system, feel free to call. We'll put one in just like mine. You'll love it.

First love

The kids and I were walking to school when Herbie spotted a letter on the ground.

Written on binder paper, it was folded up in quarters and had a slightly crumpled cast to it. As he read the letter, his smile got wider and wider. It said:

"Please read.

"Dear ... (the name has been deleted to protect the avalanche of good feeling that follows).

"I would like to know where your house is?

"I would also like to have your phone number and address please? I love you wherever you go ... Do you like horses? Do you like dogs? Do you like me? Please sign note. P.S. Thank you for reading this note."

Young romance. Don't you love it?

Well, not everyone does. And in particular, not the parents I've been talking to lately. I've promised I wouldn't use their names, but I have more than one friend who is in a complete panic over a son's or daughter's social life. It's too intense, too soon and too true-blue.

I think fifth grade is the magic age. I don't know what it is about fifth grade, but by that time children have probably seen more R-rated movies than their parents and have been less shocked by them.

I don't mean to take the innocence out of it, because basically this forest fire hasn't gotten out of control yet. This is the talking, dreaming and writing stage rather than the less-fun groping that awaits junior high students.

Don't think it isn't serious, though. Go ahead. Try to make light of it and the kids will go ballistic. They'll have their suitcases packed and in the car ready to have you drive them over to their girlfriend's. To live. For the rest of their lives.

Men, think back on your fifth- or sixth-grade flame. Maybe she wasn't your first love but it was the first time you noticed which outfits she wore that drove you crazy. How she looked when she got off the bus. The feeling of confidence when you thought she might half-stand you, too.

Mine was Nancy at William Penn Elementary School. I might have mentioned her before and if I do so again, I am going to have to start paying her residuals.

She looked great in red, fine in blue, lovely in yellow and OK in just about anything else. I was so far gone I used to come to school early so I could practice being casual when she walked on the playground.

Most of my memories of Nancy are from a distance. I was like a good field goal kicker. I was a killer from 30 yards out and a less effective short man.

I think I talked to her. In those days,

true love was consummated by holding your sweetheart's hand. We may not have gotten that far. It didn't matter. I dreamed about Nancy for years, and she became the standard for relationships later on.

I find myself teasing friends who were worried about their kids being involved with school friends. Offering advice. Putting my arm around them in that "too bad it's you, buddy" kind of way. Paper-thin sympathy.

I know it's one of those scenarios that's funny until it happens to you. The only thing I have going for me is the threat of writing about my children in the newspaper. I can always say, "You don't want me to talk about Danny in a column? Why don't we save him the embarrassment."

I have a beautiful young daughter named Katie. She is 9 and in the fourth grade. Katie still loves her mother, thinks her little brother is cute and prefers the company of little girls at cookie-decorating parties.

Friends tell me this will change. They are awaiting gleefully the time when even the threat of newsprint will do little to deter the course of Mother Nature.

I feel as though I'm out on the outer edge of the ice on a frozen lake. I know it's going to be cracking one day, but right now, it's pretty solid.

I won't be any good at it. The training you get as a child going through it is not the same training that you need as an adult watching your baby go through it.

Just blindfold me and shoot me when it happens. Katie looks terrific in red, fine in blue, lovely in yellow and OK in just about anything else, and I know one day some little boy is going to notice.

I just hope he doesn't have a good short game.

My sister Hope

There are few girls' names I like better than the name Hope. It is my younger sister's name, the sibling who moved to Norway three weeks ago with her husband and two small children.

A girl from Bakersfield by way of Boston doesn't just move to Norway. She has to have a pretty good reason, and Hope did. Her husband is Norwegian, and his father has a shipping business in Oslo.

It's hard for me not to think of Hopie as a little girl at the piano, head bent over, playing those infernal scales by the hour. The piano was a place for her to channel all the sorrow that a little girl has. I don't know where it comes from, but the sorrow is there. Fortunately with Hopie, she also has a sense of humor.

She has an explosive laugh and was funny in a way that you expect out of your brothers, not a sister. Hope's laugh starts at the top of her blond head and cascades down to her toes.

That isn't her only strength. Hope also will be remembered as a pretty fair fullback in the football games that we played in the front yard's ankle-deep sycamore leaves. She was an absolute lock to score on the short pass over the middle. She was a straight-ahead runner who disdained fancy moves. She ran, arms crossed at her chest, guarding the ball like a schoolchild hugs library books.

In college, she turned political. She was into Nicaragua before Ortega was anything but a chili sauce to most Americans. I could never understand why she was so passionate and interested in Central America. I finally understood about the time we sent troops down to Panama.

I guess even then we knew she probably wouldn't end up in this country. We thought she'd be married to a freedom fighter, so a Norwegian is not surprising. That he would be a profoundly intelligent, successful computer whiz made her parents happy, even though they now lose her to Norway.

Earlier this month, my father organized a party for her. It was a combination good-bye celebration and family reunion. Six kids, five spouses, one girlfriend, seven grandchildren. It had been a long time since we had been together.

We converged for two days at the beach. It was interesting. Big families are a perfect mirror for the world situation. There are shifting alliances, developing countries that think they know better, and then, the odd pacifist who wants no part of the battle.

The only cure for this is growing up, becoming more tolerant and, when nothing else works, living in different cities.

For one evening, we put it all aside because Hopie was leaving. And even though she is old enough to go anywhere she wants, very married with two European-looking daughters, it is not easy to move away from this country. Not easy to leave your family, and no matter how big you get, not easy to say good-bye to parents who have loved and cared for you well beyond your 21st birthday.

Even her youngest brother, Courtney, the quiet one of the lot, gave a toast. A beautiful toast where he told her how much everyone there meant to him and how much he loved his sister. Not bad from someone whom Hope used to sit on when they fought.

Sunday, the next day, people started saying their farewells. The hardest thing was watching Hope say good-bye to her older sister, Pam. Pam skirted the issue by wearing sunglasses, but they didn't cover enough of her face.

Then it was my turn. The sun was hitting Hope's face in a certain way, sending streaks of gold through her blond hair and lighting up her eyes. It was sunset light, bright red but fading to orange, and it made me think of our mortality.

You grow up with these people every day. Eat dinner with them, fight with them, sleep in the same room with them and then, one day, they're gone. But that was a long time ago.

Or was it? I can still see the determined expression on Hope's face as she broke up the middle on third and long in one of our fall football games. The way she looked on her wedding day, facing the ocean. And the sounds of the piano through the thin walls, playing out the intricacies of a young girl's soul.

Mom, the kayaker

My mom celebrated her 62nd birthday testing the Kern River in a kayak.

While many people are content marking a birthday with a restaurant dinner and cake with ice cream at home, my mother is a woman with other plans.

She's most comfortable sleeping in a one-man tent in the Alaskan outback among the grizzlies, flying fast airplanes or kayaking in rough water. As my father says, she likes to live on the outer edge of the envelope. And she's always a little surprised when people around her don't do the same.

Last week, I took her up on a long-standing invitation to go kayaking on the Kern River. It was hot out. And the Kern sounded cool.

The first thing we did was to warm up in a little pond near the river. This was easy. Glide around. Just us and the duckies.

Just you, the duckies and the giant, sucking pipe that was dragging my canoe into the sewer.

Just last week I'd heard a story about a guy in Florida who had gotten sucked into an intake valve at a power plant. Not me. I beat at the water like a crazed man and slid past the yawning hole.

A few minutes later, we loaded the kayaks in the truck and drove to the section of the river right below the Kern River Golf Course. She slid in the river and I followed her.

"Ferry across the river," she screamed, when we were both in the water. That got my attention because when my mom screams, it usually means you should have spent more time in the pond learning the Eskimo roll.

I noticed that my kayak was going down the river sideways. Having seen my share of National Geographic specials, I knew that wasn't right so I plunged my paddle into the river trying to straighten her out.

Whoops, wrong side. Now I was going backward. I righted the boat, turned downstream, only to face a cottonwood tree that had fallen into the river. I jerked across the stream to avoid its outstretched limbs. Things were happening fast.

"Rapids," she yelled cheerfully. I stiffened. No, please, not rapids.

Yep, 30 feet ahead, the sounds got shriller and the water faster as the river beat its way down a watery slope.

"Just relax," she said.

Just relax?

How? I hadn't been doing real well on the smooth water and now we were coming to the place where men go down in barrels and she wanted me to relax. It was time to sing "Nearer, My God, To Thee."

"Choose a path," she crowed.

I did. It had a big rock in it. I leaned left, I leaned right, but I kept going straight.

Scraaape. Somehow I stayed up and the boat wasn't even leaking. When I caught my breath I remembered thinking this was fun.

Fun? Never say fun your first time out in a kayak. Not because it's not fun, but because it puts an immediate hex on you.

I lost my balance and started to wobble back and forth. By the time I had righted myself, Mom was blissfully shouting, "Rapids!" again and I was slipping over them backwards.

When I had flipped my kayak around, I decided to head straight for the big rock, thinking that maybe if I aimed for it, I'd miss it. Wrong, block-head. The rock beckons, you cometh.

A few minutes later my legs fell asleep. "Mom, are your legs supposed to fall asleep like this?"

"No," she replied. "That kayak must be too small for you."

Fifteen minutes later, we floated up to the shore close to Kern River County Park. I couldn't get out of the kayak because my legs were still asleep and my arms were weak. I finally slipped over into the river, wriggled out and crawled on the bank. I reached back to drag the kayak up which, now half filled with water, weighed about 900 pounds.

Mommm-my.

She pulled her kayak out of the water and helped me with mine.

My mother is an amazing person. She gets older, she gets braver. Like Jack La Lanne, she marks birthdays with deeds, each more daring than the last.

We all like to think that when she runs out of birthdays, it'll happen front ways down a river with a full run of rapids. And she'll shoot them cheerfully, always cheerfully.

Can we go?

It might have been the Ninja Turtle movie Herbie saw for the first time this summer that quickened his interest in karate.

"I want to learn karate," he said. "I want to break bricks like Uncle Derek."

Summer's over, fall's here and it's time to figure out exactly where your children's innermost talents lie. Are they budding Leontyne Prices, miniature Peles or more compact versions of Jose Canseco?

Love is not the only motivation. It's fear. Parents quake at the thought of producing a child who cannot play at least one instrument and, an hour later, leg out a double.

At the Pearly Gates, the first question is not, "Were you good to your friends?" but "Did Tiffany learn how to play the piano?"

If the answer is no, you go to the left and help stoke the fires for the next thousand years.

Herbie wanted to learn martial arts, so I called my brother to ask his opinion. He's a black belt. My first question, left unasked, was, at what age can I expect Herbie to be kicking my tail?

"It's a great idea," he said. "Martial arts teaches them balance and coordination. Best thing in the world for a kid."

Last week we went to one of the martial arts studios to watch a class. It's easy to see why the draw is powerful.

Each of the 40 students wore a white robe. Some had matching headbands torn stylishly from towels.

The instructor was a short, powerfully built man barking out command after command to students who drank in every word.

Herbie was rapt. He couldn't take his eyes off the line of students practicing kicks and the crisp hand work.

A longish red paddle lay on the short wall separating the practice floor from the viewing area. It looked like an extra-large cribbage board with a handle. What was that for?

We found out soon enough. One of the 14-year-olds chopped right instead of left. After the boy confessed his error, the instructor went to get the paddle. He asked the student to bend over in the push-up position and then whapped him three times.

Without making a sound, the boy bowed his head and got back in line and resumed the exercises.

I looked at Herbie. The rapt expression was gone. It had been replaced by a shade of horror.

A few minutes later, a kindergartner received another light, yet distinguishable tap on the breeches. I stole another glance at Herbie. His brow was now furrowed and his thumb was in his mouth.

"Can we go?" he whispered.

I tried reasoning with him in the car. "Some of the kids weren't paying attention," I said. "The spanks weren't that hard. They didn't even cry."

He wasn't buying it. "What did they do wrong to get a spanking?" he replied.

When we got home, Herbie ran across the street to play tag with the neighbor kids. He'd rather play tag than eat.

We're really not bad parents. We just want these self-improvement classes to be cheap, in our neighborhood and only meet one day a week. And we'd prefer it if the activities weren't so life and death, either.

It would be tempting to let the whole thing slide if it wasn't for this nagging worry that somehow your kids are going to be ill-equipped in the presence of their more talented peers.

I sat on the front porch and watched the children run in the front door and out the side door of the house across the street. Tag had become hide-and-go-seek. The games were as old as childhood itself.

Herbie was right on schedule. He's doing fine at the job that requires no fancy lessons, no parent participation and no motivational speeches - just being a kid.

We'll take that any day.

Nana

This is a love letter of sorts, one that should have been written a long time ago.

A few months back, our baby sitter got sick and had to stop working. She had been coming to the house for three years. We had grown to depend on her.

Baby sitters. Want a conversation? Ask working parents with children about their child-care arrangements.

If they don't have a sitter, they are desperately trying to find one. If they do have a sitter, they're so thrilled they'll tell you everything about that person, except his or her last name.

A reliable sitter is a treasure to be protected.

Every Monday and Wednesday morning at precisely 8:30 a.m., our sitter would knock on the back door. Marge Haner, a woman in the flush of her late 60s, would ask in her Canadian accent if anyone was at home. With little fanfare, she'd come in and ask if the kids had breakfast, and if so, what. She liked to give them breakfast and always seemed a little disappointed if they had already eaten.

She instructed the kids to call her Nana. Marge was a hard name for little kids to say, she told us. Her grandchildren called her Nana and everyone liked it just fine.

Each kid was her favorite, especially at age 2. "Oh, I like that Herbie," she would say. Then later it would be,

"Katie and Herbie are wonderful, but that Sam ... "

I watched our relationship with the kids change as hers did. It was nice to know that someone was as nutty about your children as you were.

She didn't spoil them unless you count the little package of butter cookies she had in her purse each time she came. But that wasn't spoiling the children, cookies were a reward for how good they were going to be.

When the boys napped, she and Katie would have tea parties on little girl's china. When Herbie and Sam woke up, she would read them stories.

Marge was even-tempered. She didn't even get mad when she fell off the porch swing because some ninny had forgotten to secure the chain.

During Christmas two years ago, she knitted the kids little cardigan sweaters. Last year, she hooked two hanging rugs, one for Sue and me and one for Katie. Ours had a picture of flowers, and Katie's, a little girl skipping rope.

I know it sounds too perfect but it was pretty good, and pretty good is almost perfect when it comes to child care.

Call it peace of mind. Not once did I worry about the children. I'd go to work and forget the little beggars, something only the Marjorie Haners of this world can make a parent do.

When she got sick and couldn't sit

---

anymore, my wife called her on the phone. At the end of the conversation, she said, "I miss the children." Asked if she felt well enough for a visit, Marge responded, "I've lost weight. I don't want the children to see me like this."

So the kids drew pictures and sent get-well cards. Occasionally, they would ask how Nana was doing. "Is Nana going to take care of us this week?" they would ask.

Maybe next week, we'd say.

I meant to write, but you get busy and you don't do the important things.

I think about her every evening, when I put Katie to bed. I admire the hanging rug with a picture of the little girl skipping rope. It's not just the hours that she put into the rug that gets to me. It's how much she loved our children and was loved in return. No salary could have covered it, and ours certainly didn't.

We've been lucky. A woman with a Canadian accent came through our lives. She took care of our kids. She appreciated them like we did.

And I will always love her for that.

Big shot

Last weekend we went to Cambria for our once-a-year romantic getaway. WOW! WHAATT A WEEKEND.

Satisfied? Now let's get to the story.

For those who are unfamiliar with Cambria, it is a fantasylike place with lush, green ranches rolling down to some of the most pristine beaches in California. The town is filled with art galleries, quaint shops and elegant restaurants. It's a chance to be part tourist and part jolly rancher.

On Saturday - the second day of our enchanted weekend - we arranged to meet friends for dinner at a fancy restaurant. Little did they know that we planned to pick up the check. We owed them for many past kindnesses and this was our chance to reciprocate.

I had repeatedly played the scenario over in my mind. Order every appetizer on the menu, pick out the most expensive bottle of wine on the list, and when the final chord sounded, sweep up the check in a gallant gesture and take everybody's breath away.

We sat down at a beautiful corner table with a view of all the twinkly lights in Cambria. I ordered a vodka tonic just like a big shot. Then we ordered three appetizers, including crab cakes. Heck, we weren't even over $25, but who was counting?

The waitress recited the evening specials which included white sea bass, salmon and scallops in garlic sauce. Couldn't get hurt there financially, could I?

My friend ordered first, selecting the white sea bass. Capital choice. By all means. Order two if you'd like.

It was his wife's turn and she wanted ... lobster. Lobster? Lobster.

I winced. I was silent. I studied the menu and wondered how I could have missed seeing the lobster. Then I realized how. There was no price on it.

No price. Did that mean it could cost just any amount? The menu mentioned market price.

Market price. Correct me if I'm wrong, but I think market price relates to size, availability and season.

I was now in a defensive posture. I felt like the Democrats who - having to swallow a bigger defense budget than they had planned for - have to roll up their sleeves and wield the knife. My mission was to balance the check.

I studied the menu, looking for the child's plate. The restaurant didn't have one. Were they still serving breakfast? A short stack would sure taste good right now.

I looked at the wine list. Chardonnays? Forget it. We were looking at the stuff they bring in the tanker cars.

"What kind of wine would you recommend with pancakes?"

Fifteen minutes later they brought

the dinners out.

I was happy to see that the lobster fit on one plate. It wasn't the biggest lobster I'd ever seen, but it was no crawdad either. It was long, skinny and foreign-looking.

When we finished the main course, the waitress returned and asked us if we wanted dessert. Dessert? Depends on what you mean by dessert. If you're thinking about one of those things they set on fire, forget it. On the other hand, if it's a bowl of sherbet and four spoons, I might be game.

Finally, after we had chatted ourselves to death, the long-awaited check arrived. I reached for it and he reached for it. I won. Darn it.

"Why, I never expected" and "We wanted to take you out," came the protests. I waved them off. I looked at the check. Maine lobster. I was only moderately tapped.

Great weekend in Cambria. Now I know how my father feels. I guess it's about time I learned.

Reach me at the Love Castle

I went to Fike's to buy some grapefruit juice and a large apple for lunch.

Before checking out I wandered over to the meat counter. Between neatly stacked filets and thick T-bones were steaks cut in the shape of hearts.

Hmm, I thought. How about if I cooked the little woman dinner? We had friends who were going away on a ski weekend. We could use their lovely home. Farm the kids out, open a little wine and fall in love all over again.

I looked around to see if there was anybody I knew in the store. As good as that idea was, buying a piece of meat shaped like a heart is not something a he-man like me wants to advertise.

I started marinating the steak Friday night. On Saturday afternoon I loaded the car with food, mesquite charcoal and wine. I also brought a stack of our favorite albums. We might even dance a little bit. I arrived at the love castle. I unloaded the car and searched out the barbecue. The fire had to be lit for my little love steaks.

No barbecue. Unless I wanted to dig a pit, I was heading for the kitchen. What should I do? Saute the steak? Broil it? Or dip it in batter and chicken-fry it? I threw it in a cast-iron pan. After dealing with the artichokes and potatoes, I started setting the table. I laid out the good silver and went to look for the china. The cupboards held everything but dinner plates.

I went to take a shower. My lovely bride was coming over, and I wanted to look my best. I needed a shave and had bought a disposable razor to do the job. Some job. I bought the kind of razor you're supposed to throw out before you use it. My face looked like the steak I was cooking. I'd be fun to kiss if my woman was into the bleeding-fighter look.

By the time my wife arrived most of the bleeding had stopped. She looked fantastic, so we kind of balanced out. After dinner I went to put on some music. There was a turntable but no receiver. No problem - we could sit real close and read the album covers.

It was kind of a nice evening anyway. The steak was tender. The wine good. And great conversation. It flowed like Chenin Blanc. We determined that our kids were geniuses and truly extraordinary in every way. At one point, I thought we were going to order out for them.

It's an evening she will always remember. I'll tell you why. I drove her car to our dinner date and the pan holding the steak sloshed around and marinated her upholstery. She couldn't forget it if she wanted to.

Just choose me

T he big news, right along with the Pentagon scandal, is rock star Bruce Springsteen's breakup with actress Julianne Phillips.

"I feel like I got the wind knocked right out of me," my wife, Sue, said over dinner.

"I wasn't like Sandy, who thought Julianne was a bimbo in the first place and who never accepted how someone from New Jersey could be married to a lightweight from Lake Oswego. I hate to see him hurt. He's given me so much pleasure, I wish I could give something back to him."

Before I could ask exactly what that might be, she told me that I ought to check with some of his fans to see how they were taking it. Her hairdresser, Lisa, would be a good one and, of course, Sandy down in San Diego and Annie up north. All three were in their 30s with major-league Springsteen crushes.

Later that evening, Sue's sister called from Wisconsin. It turned into a sober 45-minute conversation. Judy said that she and her husband were separating. He already had moved out. Things were not good.

The only consolation, said Judy, was that Springsteen was available. And now they would have something in common.

It was clear that my wife was right about the importance of this divorce.

I called Lisa, the hairdresser, about the Springsteen breakup. She was quick to jump on the issue of Miss Phillips' lack of real committment to Bruce and his music. "She had never even seen him in concert. She had to get a backstage pass from his manager," she said with some disbelief.

"You want to know how I feel?" she asked almost defiantly. "I'm rejoicing, I'm celebrating. Now all I have to do is compete with that other redhead."

That other redhead is Springsteen's backup singer, Patty Scialfa, the woman Springsteen is rumored to have taken up with.

Lisa, the hairdresser, went on to tell me that she had first read about the breakup in National Enquirer, but she didn't believe it till she saw it in People magazine.

She also told me to call Christie, one of her clients, who is in the oil business.

"Christie has a Bruce Springsteen shrine in her office at work."

I called Christie. She was happy.

"Great move," said Christie, in what sounded like a New Jersey accent.

"Let me straighten one thing right away. I don't consider myself a fan, I'm more of a disciple."

That explained the shrine.

I asked her what she thought about Springsteen's marriage to Phillips in the first place.

"I was never for it," she said quickly

in that proprietary tone that many female Springsteen fans take. It's made up of one part maternal instinct and two parts sheer lust. "I mean that girl probably couldn't even chalk up a cue stick. She probably didn't even change her own oil." I left Christie to her shrine and called Annie from the North. Annie was not happy. She's one of these marry-them-for-life kind.

"I'm crushed that Bruce would have an affair," she whispered in a hoarse voice.

"I'm appalled, but it does shed light on his last album, which was pretty darn depressing. It also explains his latest video, which has him picking up strange women in bars."

I asked Annie if I could speak to her husband, Eric, to try to get the male point of view.

"I feel good about it," he whispered. "He's mortal after all. He's not at our level but he's closer."

Finally, I called Sandy from San Diego, who loves Springsteen more than anybody.

"He's a jerk," she said. "And I base this opinion on information from some pretty good sources."

Asked who they were, she replied, "Well, one of them was my mother."

She told me she wasn't alone amongst her friends in feeling that Bruce had screwed up. If I wanted, she could get me in touch with them.

I begged off. I already had the general drift. Bruce, I think the word's out on you. Darn it.

Don't worry,
it's just my old girlfriend

My old girlfriend came for a visit last week. I told friends at work that she was coming. Several of the men were astonished.

"I see nothing but trouble for you," one said. "What will your wife say about it?"

I tried to play sly. I told them that in my house what I say goes. I grinned, winked and acted like a 15-year-old.

What I didn't tell them was that my wife, Sue, had completely sanctioned the weekend. In anticipation of Pam's arrival on Friday night, Sue cooked a remarkable dinner: scallops and fresh tomatoes with pasta, artichokes with melted butter for dipping, pesto toast and for dessert, creme brulee.

Now what does that say about my marriage? I'll tell you. Either she is the greatest woman in the world or she has absolutely no respect for me.

The first is a given, so let's examine the second.

Some might expect her to be jealous. This is my first college girl-friend, the one I saw New York City with, the one with whom I ate dried cherries from the Italian market.

I could have gone off and settled down with this woman.

But I didn't. What I did was get married to another woman, and four kids later I'm living in Bakersfield and talking to my tomatoes.

I'm history and Pam knows it. Whoops, I meant Sue. I've got so many women with three-letter names, I can't keep them straight.

The first thing Pam told me when she arrived was that I didn't look any different. Living in Europe had been good for her diplomatic skills. Perhaps she didn't notice the hat I was wearing, covering what was once there: hair.

Pam had changed. She still had the bounce to her step but her purple high-tops that she wore to even fancy restaurants were gone. Her warmth enveloped the kids, me, Sue and the neighbors who came to join us for a glass of wine.

But 15 years after the age of 21 were not empty ones. A gifted violinist, Pam had moved to Amsterdam shortly after college for a job with an orchestra playing music for a dance company.

She had fallen in love with the first violinist, and they were married. Now, seven years later, they were divorced.

That's how she had changed. There was a little sadness around her eyes. Not crow's feet but something a little less permanent.

During dinner, we compared the last 15 years of our lives.

She talked about our neighborhood's friendliness, how lovely our children were and how nice a town Bakersfield seemed to be.

We marveled at her living in

Amsterdam and having Europe as her playground. Wouldn't it be nice to ski in the Alps, cycle around Spain and spend weeks in Paris eating French pastry?

Sometimes it helps to hear somebody else talk about your life to make you appreciate how good it is.

We talked late into the night. Gone was the tension, competitiveness and hurt of the early years after we separated. It was similar to the way I've heard people describe a 20th high school reunion.

Saturday morning, I woke up and made French pancakes. We can do Europe in Bakersfield.

We said good-bye. She headed toward Los Angeles to see cousins and explore job possibilities.

Yes, last weeked my old girlfriend came to visit. She is still the lovely, intelligent woman she was 15 years ago when we walked under a clear, breathtakingly cold Cape Cod sky. Only now, there are five more people who can appreciate her.

First kiss

I got a breathless call from Herbie, my 5-year-old son. He had something very important to tell me that couldn't wait even one more minute before he burst his britches.

"Daddy," he said, with a grin in his voice. "A little girl kissed me today."

A little girl did what? Did he know what that meant? He could be scarred for life. Worse than that, he could be awed for life.

"Tell me about it, Herbie," I said softly, careful not to get ahead of myself.

"Well," he said, starting to sound like a practiced storyteller. "It was after school. I was waiting for Mommy and this little girl, Noel, was waiting for the No. 9 bus."

I was impressed that he had remembered her bus number.

"Her bus came and she said good-bye and then she gave me a kiss."

He giggled.

I giggled.

That simple. Her bus comes, she says good-bye and she leans over as natural as can be and kisses the boy.

Where were girls like this when I was growing up? I distinctly recall having to chase Becky Gallon all over the back yard to steal a kiss. By the time I caught up with her under the pecan tree, I could barely breathe. I don't know if I kissed her or just breathed on her heavily.

That night at dinner, my wife gave me the full story. Talk about shocking revelations.

"I think there are three girls that have a crush on Herbie," she said.

I was stunned. Three girls, all in the same class. In the same school year.

"Anyway, I think this is one of the girls he's been chasing during recess," she deduced.

I asked her what he was like when she picked him up.

"You know I meet him across the street after school," she said. "This time he ran over to me and told me right away that a little girl had kissed him.

"Then he said, 'Mommy, I think it's still wet where she kissed me.' "

I asked Herbie if this was true.

He threw his head back and laughed. It was a wonderment. Here was the same child we sent to kindergarten two months ago, who wouldn't let go of his teacher's hand during recess. The one who would mysteriously turn up with a tummy ache each morning at 8 and beg us to cuddle with him.

This child, with his head back, laughing like he owned the world was not the same boy. He was stepping out.

There is a pattern in families with three kids that is as predictable as water running downhill. One child is destined to run the show, another to be in the show, and the third to steal the show.

Sometimes being in the show gets overlooked because of the brilliant direction and a riveting late entrance.

But good things happen to people who are just doing their part. Surprising things, like having a cute little girl kiss you right out of the blue. Having a mother hold your hand as you walk across the street. Having a father who loves you more than love itself.

The first kiss. What fun. I'm glad it's Herbie. His cheek will always glisten with the memory.